Rendezvous and Other Fun

By

E.Z. Chesterfield

The Night Cap

The ice in Cheryl Pak's glass rattled as she set it on the table in the back of the bar, and gave Al a playful, challenging look. Al gazed back at her over his whiskey glass, and smiled. She apparently was under the impression that, after spending all day in bed with her, his interest was waning. He chuckled to himself; they had only left the apartment because they were getting restless and needed some dinner. They had gone for sushi and were now having a night cap in a small quiet bar.

Al leaned forward, placing his hand on Cheryl's knee just below the hem of her sun dress. She smiled mischievously, pleased that her gesture had had the desired effect. Al put his mouth up to her ear and whispered "Chong-kyu". He often called her by her Korean name when he was feeling amorous.

"Yes?" she whispered back.

"Go to the lady's room and take off your panties."

"I can't do that." She replied.

"Why not?"

"I'm not wearing any."

"Chong-kyu, you are awesome!" Al whispered as he slid his hand up the inside of her thigh. She spread her legs slightly and shifted her hips a bit so his hand could reach its destination.

Al began rubbing gently. At first he was worried that he might not be able to move his hand enough to really make it work. But Chong-kyu solved the problem by slowly rocking her hips back and forth in perfect rhythm. "Mmmmm" she moaned softly, leaning against him. "Mmmmmmmmmmm!" she moaned again, resting her head on his shoulder. Al put his arm around her shoulder, pulling her close as he continued to massage her with his other hand. "Mmmmm!" she moaned yet again, then she gasped, shuddered slightly, and pressed her face against his neck.

Al looked up to see the waiter staring at them round eyed. "It's OK." Al assured him, "She's just a little tired. She'll be fine in a minute. We'll finish our drinks and go home."

The waiter nodded dubiously and moved off.

Chong-kyu giggled. But then Al applied gentle pressure and began rubbing slowly again. "Oh, baby!" she gasped quietly as she resumed rocking her hips in rhythm with his hand. "Mmmmm! Mmmm!" Al pressed a little more firmly, and Chong-kyu gasped and shuddered again. She looked up at him and said softly but urgently, "Maybe we should go back now."

Al nodded and kissed her. He helped her to her feet. She leaned against him as they walked out of the bar. "She's just a little tired." Al explained to the people at the bar who were gawking at them.

Outside, Chong-kyu had a fit of giggling.

"What's so funny?" Al asked.

"You!"

"Me?"

"I don't think you fooled anyone, saying I was tired!"

"Well, I had to say something to them. And I wanted to be sure you knew I was still interested."

"Don't worry! Your interest is showing." She said, grasping the bulge in his pants.

They arrived at her sports car. Al opened the passenger door for her and helped her into her seat. Then he walked around the car and got in the driver's seat. He started the engine, put the car in gear, and they were off.

Less than a minute later, as they motored down a quiet country road, Chong-kyu shifted slightly in her seat and said playfully "Tell me what you want to do to me when we get home."

Al smiled. He was about to say she should play with herself while he talked. But when he looked over at her, he saw there was no need for the recommendation. She had hiked her dress up just past her hips, and she had her hands buried between her legs. She gave him an angelic smile and said "Well?"

Al began a detailed explanation of how he would start kissing her on the top of her head, work his way down the back of her neck, and remove her dress as he kissed his way down her back. Chong-kyu moaned appreciatively each time he mentioned a new place he would kiss her.

Suddenly, Chong-kyu said "Turn down this road! I can't wait anymore!"

Al tapped the brakes and turned down the side road. It led back into some woods. At the first opportunity, he parked the car. He turned to her, and she threw her arms around him, saying "I want you! I really want you!"

Al put his arms around her and kissed her. He ran his hand down her back and squeezed her lovely ass.

"There's a blanket behind the seat." She said. "Let's go in the woods."

Al retrieved the blanket, and they ran into the woods hand in hand like teenage lovers. They spread out the blanket in a small clearing. Chong-kyu stepped into his arms and said again, more urgently "I want you. I really want you!" as she unfastened his pants. She slid his pants down and pulled him down on top of her as she did. He moved to begin kissing down her neck but she pulled him back up, saying "I want you! I want you now!" she whispered hotly in his ear.

He entered her and she shuddered and gasped. They kissed frantically as they made love. They held each other tight and whispered each other's names and kissed some more. When Chong-kyu began to catch her breath, Al reached down, placing the tip of his ring finger and little finger on her clit and his index and middle finger on her back door. Chong-kyu moaned happily as he applied gentle pressure. When he began rubbing, she tumbled back over the edge and began groaning and gasping again. They kept at it for a long time. When Al slowed the motion of his hand and the thrusting of his hips, Chong-kyu caught her breath. She looked up at him. He kissed her and smiled down at her.

"Are you ready, my dear?" she asked.

"I think I can go a little longer."

"Can you tell me when you're ready?"

He gave her a puzzled look.

"I want you to come in my mouth!"

Al gave a gentle appreciative laugh. "Chong-kyu, you are awesome!" he said smiling.

"But first, I want you from behind." She added with a dreamy smile.

They changed positions so that Chong-kyu was on her hands and knees. Al entered her and began thrusting slowly. Chong-kyu rocked back and forth in synch with him. He reached around with his left hand to massage her clit, and she gasped with pleasure. He ran his right hand up and down her back a few times. Then he slid his hand down her spine and pressed his thumb on her back door.

"Mmmmm!" she moaned.

He pressed again, and again she moaned. The third time he pressed she moaned again and said "in…"

The fourth time she moaned "in…please…in!", so he pressed his thumb into her back door. "Oh, Al!" she cried as it entered. "Oh! Baby!...Baby!!"

Al rocked his hips and drove deep inside her. "Oh, Chong-kyu!" he groaned.

"Oh, Al! ...mouth!"

Al slipped out of her, and scooted around as fast as he could. She grabbed him and got her mouth around him just as he came explosively. She sucked happily and played with herself enthusiastically as he shuddered and groaned repeatedly.

When he had recovered some control he looked down at her. She took his erection out of her mouth just long enough to smile at him and then began sucking gently again. "Oh, Chong-kyu, you are amazing." He said at last.

She let him go and he moved back around, lay on top of her and entered her again. He looked her in the eyes as he started rocking his hips slowly. She wrapped her arms and legs around him and pulled him close. He kissed her face and stroked her hair, and whispered her name over and over. Eventually, their hearts stopped pounding and their breathing returned to normal.

They lay in each other's arms for a long time. At last they got up and walked silently, arm in arm back to the car. Chong-kyu laid her head on his lap as they drove back to her apartment.

TREKKIES

Al had not been to a Star Trek convention in years. But Cheryl Pak loved them, and she wanted to go. And he had not seen her in about six months. So it was a grand reunion in more than one way.

Cheryl had asked him to wear his Star Trek science officer uniform when he came to visit. He had carried the blue pull over with a black collar and gold piping on the sleeve (the science uniform from the original Star Trek) in his overnight bag. And he had worn black jeans and black shoes so he could get into character quickly for her. He was not sure what she had in mind, but he figured it would be fun.

Cheryl had met him at the train station. She had on an overcoat to protect against the February wind, and underneath the coat, she was wearing the black and maroon coveralls of a Starfleet command officer (from Star Trek the next generation), complete with the four small bronze discs of a star ship captain on her collar.

After a big hug, he had looked down at her and asked "What have you got cooked up for today, young lady?"

"We're going to the Star Trek convention at the civic center." She had answered in a matter of fact way, but with a hint of mischief.

And so they had gone to the convention. It had been fun. They had stood out a bit from the crowd, being both older and more physically fit that the average Trekkie. But people took little notice of them. They had seen the display items, watched an episode on the big screen, and Cheryl had bought a new shirt for him.

"What kind of shirt?" he had asked.

"You'll see…" Cheryl had answered playfully. A short time later they left; they had seen all they wanted to see, and they were anxious to get back to the privacy of Cheryl's apartment.

Once inside the door, Cheryl pulled up a slide show on her computer and fed it into the big flat screen TV on the wall. "You can look at some pictures while I slip into something more comfortable." She explained, and then disappeared into her bed room.

The slide show began with pictures of flowers and fields, then a series of sunsets, followed by pictures of waves crashing on beaches. About the third of fourth beach photo included a young lady in a bikini. Several slides later the young ladies in the photos were topless. And a few slides after that they were fully nude. He was absorbed looking at a photo of a young lady who seemed to be having an almost sexual interaction with the surf, when he heard Cheryl's voice behind him.

"You got a package from Star Fleet." She said. She had changed into the gold velour mini skirt style uniform of a female Star Fleet officer from the original series, complete with boots, but not, he noted with interest, the customary black tights. The gold piping on the sleeves of the uniform showed two solid stripes and one dashed strip of a Captain. She set the package on the table and looked up at the flat screen TV. "What are you watching?" she demanded. "You're viewing porn? Not on MY ship you don't! Report to my office at once, mister!" She turned and strode to her office. He followed.

In front of her desk was a small carpet with two foot prints on it. He placed his feet on the prints and stood at attention.

Cheryl picked up a riding crop from her desk. She turned and glared at him. "You were probably planning to masturbate too! Weren't you?"

"No, ma'am."

"Ha! You can't fool me. Viewing porn leads to arousal, and arousal leads to masturbation. Do you know what masturbation costs this command every year? 20,000 credits! Over 400 crew members, most of them men? My quarter master tells me we go through a cubic meter of Kleenex a month! A MONTH!" She banged the riding crop on her desk for emphasis. It flew out of her hand and landed on the floor.

Cheryl bent over to pick up the riding crop. As she did, her dress hiked up, revealing her nude, perfectly shaped ass. When she stood up with the crop, her dress did not slide back down, but remained up around her hips. She stared at him. He stared at her. He couldn't help it.

"You either have a wrench in your pocket or you're aroused." She said sternly. "I intend to find out which it is." She stepped forward, grasping the front of his jeans. She unfastened them and pulled them down to his ankles. His member sprung forward, stiffening rapidly. "Hmmn!" she snorted "Just as I suspected, aroused! Step out of those pants, mister. Nothing looks more ridiculous than an officer with his pants around his ankles."

He moved to comply.

"And don't you DARE touch yourself!" she added.

"Yes, ma'am"

"What?"

"No, ma'am"

"What?"

"Wilco, ma'am"

"Well, don't just stand there!"

He got out of his pants and socks and returned to the position of attention. Cheryl paced back and forth in front of him, tapping the crop on her desk and alternately revealing her lovely garlic clove shaped ass and the beautiful little patch of glossy black hair between her legs.

She turned to face him, hands on hips. "You men and your porn and your masturbation. Ridiculous! You don't even really know how to do it properly, do you? With you it's just pump, pump, pump, pop! No beauty, no artistry, no elegance. I'll show you how it should be done!"

Cheryl walked around the side of her desk. She slipped out of her boots, and set her feet up on her desk. "Now pay attention." She commanded as she began running her hands up and down her thighs. After rubbing her thighs for a few seconds, she slipped her left hand between her legs and began rubbing slowly. With her right hand she reached up to undo the zipper so she could open the top of her dress. She slid the top of the dress down enough that she could begin massaging her breasts. "Mmmm!" she moaned, arching her back. "Ooooooooooo!" She increased the action of her hand between her legs. Soon, her moans became groans, and then gasps. She had several shuddering orgasms and then paused to rest. She looked up at him and said "Come and give me a kiss."

He stepped around the desk, knelt, and kissed her on the mouth. She smiled at him and said "Down there too." So he lowered himself down and began kissing her. She was still warm and moist from her orgasms, and it was not hard to bring her to several more. He kept kissing until she grabbed him by the ears, pulled him up, and kissed him on the mouth. "Go open your package from Star Fleet." She said, trying to sound stern, but just sounding dreamy.

He stood and walked back to the living room, where the package still sat on the table. He felt light headed, and the pressure in his groin was almost painful. He opened the package. It contained a letter and the shirt Cheryl had bought him. The letter read "Effective immediately, you are promoted to the rank of Commodore. You are to assess the health of the Captain at once." He looked at the shirt. It bore the single wide stripe of a Star Fleet Commodore on each sleeve. He smiled as he slipped off his old shirt and donned the new one.

When he stepped into her office, Cheryl looked up at him wide eyed, saying "Commodore, I had no idea!"

"It's quite alright, Captain. But I must tell you that I have diagnosed your condition. I have found that you suffer from…   …phallic hostility."

"Is it serous?"

"Quite serious"

"Will I be punished?"

"No, but therapy is urgently required."

"I'll do whatever is needed, Commodore."

"Good. The medical journals call for fellatio/masturbation therapy."

"I see. What do I need to do?"

He walked around the side of her desk and sat on the edge in front of her. "You are to play with yourself as you fellate me." He explained. "It is believed that the act of fellatio, coupled with the pleasure of masturbation will cure you of the hostility."

"I see! I hope it works." Cheryl said, slipping her right hand between her legs. She grasped him with her left hand and brought her mouth down onto his now throbbing erection. She sucked eagerly, slowly at first, but speeding up, and playing with herself all the while. Soon she was climaxing again, moaning and having to take his erection out of her mouth to be sure she didn't bite it.

After her climax, she sucked and stroked happily and vigorously. When his breathing became irregular, she just picked up the pace.

He grunted and the first shot went into the back of her mouth. She pulled back involuntarily, and the second shot hit her in the face. The third and fourth landed on her breasts. She managed to get her mouth back on him in time to catch the fifth, as well as the aftershocks, in her mouth. She hummed happily and sucked a little more.

Cheryl looked up at him. It was a few seconds before he was even able to return her gaze. She smiled and said "I'm sorry I couldn't get it all in my mouth, Commodore."

"That…   …that's quite all right." He said with a breathless laugh. Then he added. "You may go and take a shower."

She stood up, gave him an angelic smile and a kiss on the forehead, and walked to the bathroom with her hips swaying.

"I'll join you in a minute." He said still catching his breath.

"Sounds delightful" she replied.

Cheryl had almost finished washing, and the shower was full of steam, when he entered the stall. She stepped into his arms. "Mmmm, that was really fun." She said.

"Yes," he said, kissing her and hugging her, "Yes, it was."

They washed each other. They dried each other. They went to the bed and made love all night long.

The Nature of the Lady

Al held his cell phone at arm's length and glowered at it. It was at times like these that he had to remind himself of the nature of Cheryl Pak and the nature of their friendship. It was not that she didn't want to talk to him. She was just busy. And it was not just her. She had asked him to call late Tuesday night, but he had been stuck in a late meeting at the factory and had not been able to call. So now it was Thursday, and though they had planned to chat, he kept getting her voice mail. Dang!

He tossed his phone on the bed and went to take a shower. As he washed, he tried to think about work and not fume over the missed opportunity to chat. It was always fun chatting with her; she was delightful company, even over the phone. This thought put him in a good mood, and he finished his shower with a smile.

His cell phone was ringing as he shut off the water. He moved quickly, but by the time he got to the phone, he had missed the call. Sure enough, it had been Cheryl. He recognized her Skype number. But he could not call in to Skype, so he called her Blackberry again. No answer. Had she left her Blackberry at work? Unknown. But it was clear that the call for tonight was off. Crap!

Al waked back to the bathroom and dried himself off. He returned to the bed and tried to read. But his thoughts kept returning to the missed call. It really would have been fun to talk. Oh, well, it would work out in the end. When they finally talked it would be great. And when they finally saw each other again, it would be great too. It always was. It was not often that they saw each other, and took a lot of effort to make it happen. But when they did…it was astoundingly fun.

He thought back over the years they had known each other. Had it always been good? It had. Even their worst meeting still made him laugh. It had been pretty tense at first, but it had ended well. And it had given him a glimpse into her enigmatic personality.

They had met for the first time at a trade show. His company made medical devices, and her company used them. She had stopped by his company's booth, looking for blood gas analyzers. He knew all about them, having been on the team that designed them and brought them to market. He had explained them, she had listened and asked very perceptive questions. And there was something about the way she observed, and spoke, and even carried herself; a quiet intensity behind the mild, almost unreadable mannerisms. He found himself asking her to have coffee with him later, and was surprised when she agreed. By the end of the show, there was clearly something cooking between them. But by the time they came to that realization, they had checked out of their hotel rooms. There was no where they could go to be alone together.

"There is another trade show in February. How about then?" he had suggested.

"Perfect!" she answered with a mischievous smile. "February then!"

But in January the economy tanked, there were lay-offs, his company was not sending anyone to trade shows, and he did not dare take vacation. He sent her an email apologizing. "No worries. Later then." she had responded. She was not given to verbosity.

They planned to meet in New York. But that visit got scotched when she got a job promotion and had to work through the weekend. He almost couldn't believe it. If it had been anyone else, he would have thought she was avoiding him. But avoidance was not her style. If she did not want to see him, she just would have said so. And anyway, she had called a few weeks later and had been very sweet. She had also been very plain about the fact that she still wanted to see him. So it was still on. And they made plans to meet in Chicago in July. She had a conference there, and he took a few days off from work, his long overdue vacation, to travel out and see her.

It had been a tough visit. She could not get away from her conference for more than a few hours each day, and while he understood, he was also a bit annoyed at having crossed half a continent to see her only to be limited to a few hours of her time. The fact that she was having her period had not helped either.

And so they lay on the bed, in his hotel room, she feeling tense and he feeling frustrated, joking and trying to make the best of it. Finally, she had looked at him with concern. "Are you OK?" she asked.

"Yeah, just…"

"I know, I'm sorry. It's just weird for me. I'm in your hotel room. I don't do this sort of thing!"

"It's OK. It's nice to see you anyway. You are delightful company, even if we can't make love."

"Ooooh, you're sweet!" she said, and lay her head back down on his shoulder.

He stroked her hair.

She raised her head back up and looked at him with a hint of mischief in her eyes. He looked back and raised his eyebrows in question. She smiled and said "Do you want to come, baby?"

"Huh?"

"Here," she said, unfastening his pants, "let me do this for you."

"OK…"

She got his pants out of the way and started massaging him. "Hmm, nice!" she said happily.

"Are you going to kiss it?" he asked.

"Next time" she assured him, "for now, just lay back and relax."

So he had lain back and relaxed. And she had worked with a skill and enthusiasm he could hardly believe. Hand jobs are the consolation prize of sex. They are often given grudgingly. But this was different. She gave him a hand job that was better than some of the blow jobs he had gotten. As he arched his back and groaned, she had picked up the pace and kept it up even as he came explosively.

"Oh, I made a mess of your shirt! Sorry!" she had said with a laugh.

"Quite all right!" he laughed "Wow!"

"Did you like it?"

"Yes!" He climbed out of bed, rolled his shirt as he took it off, tossed it in the corner, and fished a new shirt from his bag. "That was something else!"

She smiled at him. "Would you be disappointed if I said I had to go?"

"A bit. It seems a shame, just when things were getting so interesting."

"Next time. OK?"

"OK"

She got up and began putting on her dress. He watched her. She looked over at him. "What?"

"There is one other thing." He said, rising and putting his arms around her.

"What is it, my dear?"

"It may sound crazy, but I believe I love you."

"Mmm, I love you too." She said happily. She kissed him and added. "I really have to go. Let's meet again soon. OK?"

He nodded. They had a big hug. She left.

They had met again. It hadn't been soon, but it had been wonderful.

What Goes Well with Coffee

A street sweeper machine drove past. Al looked up from under the hood of his classic car. He smiled. They were taking the salt off the road. Pretty soon he would be able to drive his car without worrying about rust. He wiped his hands on a rag and stepped away from the car. He pulled out his smart phone and checked the weather report. His smile widened. Better and better; there was going to be three days of rain during the week. By next weekend the roads would be completely clean. His smile widened further. He had a good idea. He sent a text to Cheryl Pak. Then he returned to working on the car. He needed the car running, and running well, by next weekend.

In the evening, after taking a shower, Al leaned back on his bed and called Cheryl. He was half expecting she would be too busy to take a call, she often was, so he was caught a bit off guard when she answered.

"Hi, Al, what's up?"

"Ah…hi…just calling to see if you got my text."

"I got a text, but I did not have time to check it. Was it from you?"

"Of course, that's why I called."

"So what's up?"

"Well, the roads have been swept, and it is going to rain next week, so I was thinking of taking a road trip next weekend."

"Oh, cool! Can you come out this way?" Cheryl asked hopefully.

"That's what I was thinking…"

"Yay!"

"So I was thinking I could drive out Friday night, we could spend the weekend together, and I can drive back Sunday night. How does that sound?"

"Ah…I don't know…"

"Huh?"

"I have this major presentation I need to get ready."

"I thought you wanted to see me."

"I do! I really do. I just can't commit to a whole weekend."

"What can you commit to?"

"I'm not sure."

"Cheryl…come on, you must have some idea!"

"OK, I can commit to one hour, just for you."

"One hour?"

"Just for you"

"One hour? Really?"

"How about *at least* one hour?"

"Cheryl, some people would consider that more of an insult than an invitation."

"Come on baby, don't be like that. I want to see you. I really do. It's just that my new job is crazy busy."

"Hmm"

"I'll have the coffee pot on. I know you like my coffee."

"Uh huh?"

"And I'll make the trip worthwhile. I can promise one other thing that I *know* you'll like!"

"Cheryl, I am not driving five hours just for a cup of coffee and a blow job!"

"No?"

"Well…now that I think of it, maybe it is worth the trip for one of your blow jobs."

"Yay!"

"It would be nice to spend more than an hour though…"

"I know…" Cheryl sounded pained. "I wish we had more time too! I want some of your kissing. I really like the way you kiss. But I can only commit to an hour. I don't want to promise something I can't deliver. You understand?"

"Sure. And as I think about it, it is a pleasant thought: coffee and a blow job."

"Yay! I promise not to disappoint!"

"I know you won't."

"Hey, can I call you later? I am getting a call on the other line."

"OK"

"Kisses!"

"To you too."

"Bye!" Cheryl broke the connection.

Al stared at his phone and snorted, 'Crazy Lady!' he thought. Still, he had to smile.

*   *   *   *

All week long, Cheryl worked on her presentation and the other things her boss threw mercilessly at her. Just when she thought she had gotten far enough ahead to spend all of Saturday afternoon and night with Al, something else came up. She liked the job, it was fascinating, but sometimes she missed the days when she and Al could go to Star Trek conventions together and spend entire nights of passion and romance. But, well, this job would not last forever; it was a stepping stone to a more interesting, and less time consuming position that she really wanted. Then there would be more time for fun. For now, work and more work, and grab a bit of fun when it was available. Thank goodness Al understood.

Saturday morning she had planned to get up early. She still had to do the final edits on the presentation. But she had left her phone in the other room, so she did not hear the alarm or the two calls from Al that morning. She called Al back, but he didn't answer. 'He must be driving.' she thought.

After a quick shower, Cheryl put on a silk camisole and a pair of lace panties, wrapped a robe around herself, set up the coffee maker, and started her computer. Maybe she could get some work done before Al arrived. As it turned out, she had a couple of hours. She was so deeply focused on her work when Al arrived that it took her a moment to realize her door bell was ringing.

She looked out the window and saw Al's car in the drive way. She made a quick wardrobe adjustment, and went to answer the door.

Al looked happy, but a bit impatient, when she opened the door for him. No matter, she knew exactly how to improve his mood. She gave him a big hug and led him into the living room of her apartment. "Take off your coat and get comfortable, baby." she said playfully.

Al took off his coat and hung it on the back of a chair. He turned to look at her, and Cheryl undid her robe and let it fall open.

"Oh, Chong-kyu, you are awesome!" he said with a big smile. Cheryl was not wearing any panties.

"Get comfortable on the couch, my dear." she said.

"Should I take off my pants?" he asked.

"If you like…"

"Should I take off my underpants as well?" he asked as he undid his belt.

"If you like…"

Al sat on the couch. Chong-kyu smiled at his stiffening member, hummed happily, stepped forward, knelt between his legs, and took him in her mouth.

"Wow!" Al said. Chong-kyu began sucking and stroking. Al groaned softly, then he said "Hey, baby, why don't you play with yourself while you do that?"

Chong-kyu took him out of her mouth for a second to say "OK!" and resumed kissing. She also began rubbing herself. "Mmmm" she moaned.

Al ran his hand through her hair. "I want to kiss you too, my treasure!"

"Oh, nice!" she said. She sat next to him on the couch and then leaned back. Al wasted no time. He buried his face between her legs and began kissing vigorously. Chong-kyu gasped with pleasure. Al massaged her smooth shapely thighs with his hands as he kissed. Occasionally, as he massaged her thighs he would bring his hand down to rub and squeeze her perfectly shaped ass. When he did, Chong-kyu threw her head back and groaned with pleasure. Al kept at it, pressing relentlessly and kissing tirelessly. Soon Chong-kyu was howling with ecstasy. Still, Al kept kissing. Chong-kyu squeezed his head between her thighs. Al could not move his head, so he stopped kissing for a moment, though he kept massaging her thighs and ass. Chong-kyu regained he composure long enough to pull Al's hand to the center of her fabulous ass. She heard him chuckle slightly in anticipation, and she relaxed her thighs. Al began kissing again, squeezed her ass, and pressed his thumb against her back door.

"Oh, Al! Oh, baby! OH, Al, baby!" she cried. Still, Al kept kissing. If anything, he became more enthusiastic, kissing her pussy and pressing on her back door. "Al, baby…in! Please, IN!" she groaned.

Al pushed his thumb gently into her back door. He kissed with still more enthusiasm, and Chong-kyu threw her head back again and howled. "Ohh! Ohhh!! OOOHHH!" With the last shout, she felt herself gush all over his face. "Oh, Al, baby!" she gasped. She ran her hand into his hair and pulled him gently up so that she could kiss his face.

She kissed him and said "Al, baby, let me rest a second, OK?"

Al nodded. "I should wash my face." He said. "And my hand too." He added as he slowly withdrew his thumb from her back door. He kissed her again and then went to the bathroom to wash up.

Chong-kyu sighed and lay back on the couch, drifting along in a haze of happiness and pleasure. She looked over at Al, who was stepping back out of the bathroom, and smiled contentedly.

Then her work phone rang.

Cheryl felt like screaming. Instead, she answered the phone. "Hello, this is Cheryl."

"Cheryl, it's Linda. I thought you were going to have that presentation ready by 2PM."

"It will be."

"Cheryl, it's 2:05 now."

"Oh, I'm sorry. A friend called, I lost track of time. I will send it in fifteen minutes."

"There's one other thing. I need you to come in to the office. The customer wants to see it in person. Can you be here by 3:00?"

"Umm, 3:00. Yes, I should be able to be there in time."

"Don't be late. This is important."

"OK"

"See you then." Her boss said, and hung up.

Cheryl looked up to see Al standing before her, looking almost crestfallen. She could not let him down. He had driven all the way to see her, which was sweet. Besides, she thought, looking at his semi erect cock, it was so much fun playing with him. "Al, baby, don't worry. I didn't forget you. Sit down here and let me give you a hand job."

"A hand job?" Al asked, sitting down. "I was kind of hoping for a blow job."

"Blow jobs take too long, baby." She said, grabbing his cock and starting to stroke. Let me give you a hand job. They're faster, and still a lot of fun."

"Hmm," Al said, still not fully satisfied, but starting to relax, and clearly enjoying Cheryl's skill as she worked her hand up and down. "Could you at least kiss it a little?"

"Oh, sure!" Chong-kyu said happily. She leaned over and started sucking as she pumped with her hand.

Al groaned "Oh, Chong-kyu, you are amazing!"

She raised her head, smiled at him, and kissed his cheek, all the while enthusiastically pumping his erection. Then she brought her mouth down on it again and kissed with her customary joyous enthusiasm. She lifted her head again and asked "Are you about ready to come, baby?" as she scooted around to kneel on the floor between his legs.

Al just nodded.

"Do you want to come in my mouth?"

Al nodded again.

Chong-kyu smiled and then started sucking again. She took a deep breath through her nose, opened the back of her jaws and slid her head down all the way so she could deep throat him. That was all it took. Al groaned and came hard, arching his hips. Chong-kyu pulled back a little so that she got at least some of it on her tongue. She sucked a little more and then raised her head. "How was that, my dear?"

"Wow!" was all Al could say.

She laid her head on Al's knee and felt him run his hand affectionately through her hair. It was so nice making each other happy.

Then she saw the clock on the table. Oh, no! She was going to be late again. And she might make Al sad in the process. But there was no way around it. She raised her head and said. "Al, baby, I have to get dressed now. Could you turn on the coffee maker so we can at least take coffee with us as we head out?"

Al nodded.

"Are you mad?"

"No…I just wish we had more time."

"I do too!" she said. Then, yielding to the tight schedule, she got up and went to get dressed.

When she got down stairs, she found that he had gotten dressed as well, and was pouring two cups of coffee in travel mugs. "Do you want cream in your coffee, my treasure?"

"Just black is fine." She answered, and then added playfully "I already had my cream!"

"Ah, Chong-kyu, you are awesome!"

They took their coffee out to the parking lot. They had one more hug. Then they got in their cars. Cheryl headed for her office. Al headed to the highway.

Mirror

It was thirst that finally made her get out of bed. Chong-kyu did not want to get out of bed, she felt so comfortable in his arms. Still, the thirst was nagging. And she would only be away a moment.

Slowly she disentangled from him. He muttered in his sleep. She kissed him. He smiled and was quiet.

She walked to the bathroom. After two glasses of water, she felt better. In fact, with the thirst gone, she felt what she had been feeling all weekend. She felt wonderfully rested and wonderfully relaxed. Along with rested and relaxed, she felt beautiful, just amazingly beautiful.

On the way back to the bed, she stopped, turned gracefully, and gazed at herself in the full length mirror. But the image she saw was just her, just Cheryl. Pretty perhaps but… …but…

But Al always told her "Chong-kyu, you are so beautiful!" She smiled at the thought. And then WHAM! She suddenly saw herself as he saw her; beautiful, radiant, transcendently lovely. She gasped softly.

"Chong-kyu," she heard him say "what's up?"

She turned and saw him standing there, smiling at her. She threw herself into his arms.

"Wow!" he said in delighted surprise "What did I do to earn such a magnificent hug?"

"Mmmmmmm!" she explained.

"Mmmm, Mmm, Mmm, Mmm!" Al agreed, holding her tight and kissing her.

They strayed like that for a while. Then Chong-kyu asked "Do you know what time it is?"

"I haven't been paying attention to the time." Al replied.

"Mmmm, me either…   …just drifting along"

"It looks like it's getting close to dawn." Al said, gazing out the hotel window.

"Should I make some coffee? We could have breakfast on the balcony and watch the sun rise."

Al kissed her and nodded.

They went to the kitchen. Al made coffee. Chong-kyu toasted English muffins. They brought them to the balcony and set them on the low table. There was a love seat; wicker with all-weather cushions. They sat side by side, pressing against each other for warmth, and also because they enjoyed it.

They munched on the English muffins and sipped their coffee as the sky over the ocean slowly turned a lighter grey. Chong-kyu leaned on Al and said "It's nice having breakfast and watching the sun rise."

"Mmmm"

"You know what else might be nice?" she asked playfully.

Al smiled broadly. "I certainly do!"

Al kissed her and stood up. He reoriented the love seat while Chong-kyu slipped out of her panties. Glancing at the brightening horizon, he stepped out of his shorts and said "We'll have to get ready quickly."

"I think we can manage." Chong-kyu said with happy confidence. She knelt on the love seat and leaned forward, resting her elbows on the railing of the balcony. She reached over, grasped Al and began playing with him.

Al ran his hand up and down her back and then began massaging her shapely derriere. She moaned softly, and he ran his hand between her legs. He began rubbing and she moaned again.

Chong-kyu looked over and admired the results her handy work. "I want to kiss you." she said with her usual mischievous smile. Al stepped forward so she could kiss him. He kept massaging her, even as he marveled at the skill and enthusiasm of her kissing. The fact that she was moaning with pleasure the whole time made it all the more fabulous.

After a minute or so, with the eastern sky becoming quite light, she took him out of her mouth and said "Al, baby, I think I'm ready."

He moved around behind her, all the while massaging her derriere. Chong-kyu gasped as he entered her slowly. "Oh, baby!" she cried as he began moving in and out of her. He ran his hands up and down her back, massaged her derriere, squeezed her breasts, rubbed her stomach and thighs. She cooed happily each time his hands found a new place on her body.

As much as the pleasure, the thrill of making love out on the balcony, and the romance of doing it as the sun rose, carried her away. "Oh, Al, Baby!" she moaned. He drove deeply but gently inside her, kissing her from the inside, and his hands found exactly the right spot on her body. She tried to call his name again, but all that came out was a great joyful cry as she shuddered. She was not sure how long it went on, but it was quite a bit lighter when she opened her eyes.

Al was still rocking his hips and pressing deep inside her, but her head was clear enough that she could make out the sound of voices that seemed to be chanting rhythmically. She looked around, and spotted, down in the parking lot, a group of college kids. They had, no doubt, just come back from and all night party, and were now standing, staring, and cheering them on.

Her next cry of pleasure mixed with a laugh and came out like a hiccup. Then she laughed again and looked over her shoulder at Al.

Al grinned and bobbed his eyebrows up and down. He seemed very pleased with himself.

"Al, baby" she said a bit breathlessly.

"Yes, my treasure?"

"Baby, come up here and sit on the railing."

"Now?"

"Mmm, it's getting too light, and I thought we could have a grand finale for our fans" she said playfully.

Al slid out of her. He rubbed her derriere as he walked up and sat on the railing.

Chong-kyu grasped him with her left hand. She gave the audience a wink, a thumbs-up, and a smile. She began kissing Al, slipping her right hand between her legs so she could play with herself as she kissed. She had to take him out of her mouth several times when the excitement got overpowering. But when she sensed he was near the edge, she picked up the pace and really concentrated on the kissing. She kept at it until he started coming, pulling him out of her mouth quickly as he groaned and called her name. She pressed him against her cheek so that he came all over her face.

"Oh, Chong-kyu!" he gasped as he came.

"Yay!" she cheered.

The fans in the parking lot cheered too.

She gave him one more, quick kiss. She waved at the fans, blew them a kiss, and waved again before she and Al walked back into the hotel room.

"Chong-kyu, you are amazing!" Al said, as he ran the shower to warm it up and Chong-kyu wiped her face with a towel.

"That wasn't too slutty?" she asked playfully.

"In someone else, it might be slutty. With you, it's just sweet and crazy. Mostly sweet"

In the shower they held each other for a long time. Then they washed each other, dried each other, and returned to the bed, where they held each other some more. Chong-kyu lay on top of him, sighing as he ran his hand up and down her back and occasionally kissed the top of her head.

"Al, baby?"

"Yes, my treasure?"

"Are you sure that wasn't too slutty?"

Al looked at her. He smiled and kissed her forehead. "Chong-kyu, my treasure, there is nothing slutty about you. You are just fun and wonderful." He kissed her again for emphasis.

"Mmmm" Chong-kyu said, squeezing him. He squeezed back, and they both broke out laughing.

A while later, Chong-kyu raised her head. "Are you hungry, my dear?" she asked.

"A little"

She rolled over and grabbed the phone. She called the front desk. "Hi, this is Cheryl Pak in room 302. I'd like to order breakfast from room service... ...Oh, I see. OK, no worries." She hung up the phone.

Al raised his eye brows.

"They don't have room service."

Al nodded and kissed her fore head.

"Are you in a hurry for breakfast?"

Al shook his head.

Chong-kyu laid her head on his chest again and sighed. Al ran his hand up and down her back. Aside from an occasional bought of laughter, they mostly just lay silently in each other's arms.

The sun was high in the sky and very warm when they finally got out of bed, pulled on some clothes, and went looking for breakfast. They found a place that served Champagne Brunch. It seemed about right, so they went in and got a table.

They had finished their eggs and were working on their toast and sipping coffee when the waiter approached. He was carrying a bottle of champagne. "From the… …gentlemen… …at the corner table." He explained, gesturing with a nod of his head.

The kids from the parking lot grinned and waved at them. Al and Chong-kyu waved back. Al popped open the bottle, poured them two glasses, and they raised their glasses in a toast. The kids clapped and cheered.

Chong-kyu leaned forward. She gave Al a sweet smile and said "Shall we go back to the room?"

Al smiled back and said "There's nothing I'd like better."

Phone Calls

The phone rang several times. Al was about to hang up. It was his third call to Cheryl that evening, and it looked like he would not be getting through. But just as he was getting ready to end the call, he heard "…hello?"

"Cheryl?"

"Oh, hello, my dear!"

"Hey, how've you been?"

"Busy…crazy busy. Sorry I couldn't answer the phone earlier. Sales meeting…"

"That's fine. Have you a moment now?"

"Just a moment, can I call you later?"

"Ah…sure…what time?"

"I don't know, probably late. Will you be up?"

"Sure, call any time. I'll turn up the ring tone so it wakes me."

"OK, sounds good! Chat later! Bye!"

"OK, bye" Al reached to end the call, but Cheryl had already disconnected. He shrugged and put the phone away. It was time to get some dinner anyway. He grabbed his brief case and headed down to the hotel bar.

As he munched his chef's salad (a nod to Cheryl, who was, among other things, a dietician) and sipped his ice tea, Al read through the report the supplier had given him. He was in town doing evaluations on some alloy samples. The alloys represented coatings and substrates for blood analyzers his company made. The coatings had to react correctly with certain chemicals in the blood. The substrates, by contrast, must not react with either the blood or the coating. It was a harder trick than it looked at first. So he had been sent out by his company to assist the supplier in developing the alloys. It was interesting stuff. He jotted down a few ideas as he read and ate.

Afterwards, he tried watching some football on the TV above the bar. But his mind kept drifting to the prospect of the phone call with Cheryl. If she called, it would surely be great fun. His mind drifted back to the first of their late night calls.

They had spoken on the phone a few times, and it was always nice. Just some friendly conversation, planning places they could go together, discussions of their respective jobs, nothing more. But one night, she had started asking more intimate questions.

"What is the wildest thing you ever did?" she had asked.

"I guess racing my car at the old industrial park back in high school."

"I mean, what is the wildest thing you ever did in bed?"

"Oh, come on, you don't really want to know."

"Yes, I do!"

"You'll feel jealous."

"I'm not the jealous type."

"Emotions are unpredictable."

"Come on, tell me."

"You first."

"No, you first. I asked first. Tell me!"

"Are you sure you want to hear?"

"Yup!"

"OK, one time this old girlfriend of mine and I made a sex tape."

"Really? What was it like?"

"Well, we set the camera on a tripod, and we did an 'around the world', and caught it on tape. It actually didn't come out all that great."

"What's an 'around the world'?"

"Well…are you sure you want to hear this?"

"Yes! Tell me."

"OK, so we started out with just her on the bed. She got out of her clothes, and began masturbating."

"Mmmm, sounds nice. Go on."

"So then I walked on camera…"

"Were you naked?"

"Yes"

"Nice…and?"

"And so I started kissing her."

"Where?"

"All over her body. But eventually, of course, I started kissing between her legs."

"Nice!"

"And then after a while she started sucking me. And we did a 69 for a while."

"Nice…then what?"

"Well, then we started making love. And we did that for a while."

"How long?"

"Not that long, a few minutes. Remember, we were going for entertainment value, not maximum pleasure. We had a few more things to get through before the climax."

"Really? Like what?"

"Well, after making love for a bit, I slipped out, and she positioned herself on her side, with one leg in the air, and…I, ah…"

"You what?"

"I put on a condom and…ah…entered her back door."

"Oh, wow! Did it hurt?"

"She said it didn't. Well, she said it did at first, but we did a few rehearsals, and she said that by the third time it actually felt pretty good. So…"

"I see…"

"So, anyway, we did that for a bit. Then we stopped the camera. I took off the condom, washed, just in case, restarted the camera, and I…ah…we…did the grand finale."

"Did you come on her face?"

"Um…yes…how did you know?"

"I've seen those movies before. I don't really like them, but I know what happens. Anyway, it sounds like it was a lot of fun."

"It was fun. So how about you?"

"What?"

"Your turn to tell about the wildest thing you did in bed."

"Oh, one time Reggie, my old boyfriend, and I made love in the middle of the afternoon with the windows open. I am pretty sure the neighbors heard us."

Al had been surprised to feel a brief jolt of jealousy. Why had he felt jealous of Cheryl's ex-boyfriend? He had shaken off the unworthy feeling, chuckled and said "That's pretty cool. But why did you want to swap these stories anyway?"

"I just want to be sure we can talk about anything together. It seems special."

"Hmm, I guess that makes sense. Was there anything else you had in mind?"

"Well…can I ask you a question?

"Sure!"

"Do you ever touch yourself?"

"Huh?" Al asked, laughing.

"Do you ever touch yourself?"

"Cheryl, I'm a guy. Of course I do."

"Want to hear a secret?"

"Sure"

"I'm doing it now!"

"What?"

"I'm doing it now!"

"Wow! That's so sweet! I feel honored."

"Honored? Not excited?"

"Honored and excited. I guess it is special that we can talk about anything together."

"Don't you want to do it too?"

"What?"

"What do you think, silly? Play with yourself!"

"Um…"

"Come on, I want you to do it!"

"OK…"

"Are you playing?"

"Yes…"

"Good! Now, tell me what you want to do to me when we are together."

And he had, and it had been great fun. And they had done it a few more times. They did not always have phone sex when they talked, and it was hard to tell when Cheryl would be in the mood for it. But when she was, it was very hot.

Al was hoping that she would be in the mood tonight. It would be OK if she wasn't; it was fun talking anyway. But if she was in the mood…

Al realized that the bar tender was asking him if he wanted a refill of ice tea. He shook the foolish grin off his face and said "No thanks, just the check please."

*

Back up in the room, Al took a shower, dried, and tried calling Cheryl. No answer. He grunted and got into bed. He tried reading, but could not concentrate. He turned off the light and went to sleep.

The phone woke him up. He did not stop to check the time. He just answered it as quickly as possible.

"Hello?"

"Hello, baby. How are you?"

"Fine, how are you?"

"I'm good. What are you doing?"

"I'm lying in bed talking with you. What are you doing?"

"I'm playing…"

"Ah, Chong-kyu, you are awesome!"

"And I want you to play too!"

"OK" he said. He slid his pants down, grabbed his slowly stiffening member, and began stroking.

"Are you playing now?"

"Yup"

"Nice, so tell me what you want to do when we get together."

"Shall we take a shower together?"

"Nice, would you like me to suck your cock in the shower?"

"Sure, should I kiss your pussy?"

"Mmm, nice!"

And so it went for about twenty minutes, with Cheryl occasionally saying "Oh my gosh!" as she had mini orgasms. Finally, she said "Hey, baby, are you ready to come?"

"Sure"

"Let's come together. Tell me how you want to come with me."

Al did his best to describe making love with her in a lounge chair by the side of a pool at midnight. He tried to keep it from being too repetitive, and keep it interesting but not too complicated. It worked, he heard Cheryl gasping and keening. He stopped talking so as not to distract her from her orgasms.

"Did you come, baby?" she asked.

"Not yet" he admitted.

"We were supposed to come together!" she said, slightly disappointed.

"Sorry"

"No worries. But I want you to come now. Tell me what you want to do to me."

"I have been…"

"Tell me what will make you come."

"Well…"

"Do you want to fuck me in the ass?" she asked playfully.

"Yeah, that sounds fun."

"OK, baby, come on, fuck me in the ass!"

"OK, here it is, raise your legs above your head and I'll slip it in."

"Are you playing?"

"Of course!"

"Nice, now imagine you're fucking me in the ass while you play!"

"Oh, yeah!"

"Are you ready to come?"

"Yup, where should I come?"

"Anywhere you want, baby."

"Should I pull it out and come on your ass?"

"Sounds hot! Come on, baby let me hear you come!"

"OK, you want it? Here it comes!" he groaned, and shot a load onto the hotel sheets.

"Did you come?"

"Uh huh!"

"Nice! Was it fun?"

"Of course. How about you?"

"It was really fun! Hey, it's getting late. We better get some sleep!"

"OK…"

"Chat soon, baby! Good night!"

"Uh…good night…"

Cheryl hung up the phone.

Al shook his head. "Crazy lady!" he thought with a smile. He rolled out of bed, got some towels from the bathroom, and cleaned up the bed. When he climbed back into bed, he fell asleep almost instantly.

He woke up with a start when he recognized Cheryl's ring tone. He grabbed the phone and answered it.

"Hello?"

"Hey, baby, I wanted to talk some more." Cheryl said.

"Is that your toy I here buzzing?"

"Yes"

"Oh, Chong-kyu, you are awesome!"

"I know! Now listen while I tell you my fantasy!"

"OK!"

"Oooo, I have you in my pussy and him in my mouth. Mmmm, now he's in my pussy and you're in my back door! Oh my gosh!"

"Who is he?" Al asked, a bit startled.

"No one in particular. I just want to fantasize about manage a trois. Do you mind?"

"Ah, no…"

"Oh, good. Oooo, now you in my mouth and him in my pussy, oh yeah! Oh my gosh! Him in my pussy and you in my back door again. Oooo manage a trois. Oh my gosh! Him in my mouth and you in my pussy! Oooo manage a trois. Oh my gosh! Oh, baby, are you hard again?"

"I'm getting hard…"

"Come on baby, play with yourself!"

"OK. I'm stroking. I'm imagining driving deep in you pussy while you kiss some girl's big boobs."

"I'm not a lesbian. I don't want to kiss a pussy."

"Not her pussy, her boobs."

"No, just listen. I want to tell you my fantasy."

"OK"

"Mmm, now you in my mouth and him in my pussy…mmm…him in my pussy and you in my back door… Oooo manage a trois. Him in my mouth and you in my pussy. Oh my gosh! Oh yeah! Now him in my mouth and you in my back door! Oh my gosh! Oh, BABY! OH my gosh!"

"Did you come baby?"

"Mmm, I did, but I want to come again before you hang up!"

"Sure, as many times as you want!" Al was impressed and pleased that Chong-kyu was having such fun.

"Oooo manage a trois! Oh my gosh! Him in my pussy and you in my mouth. Oooo now you in my pussy and him in my back door. Oooo manage a trois. Oh, yeah! You in my mouth and him in my pussy. Oooo manage a trois. Oh my gosh!"

"You're really having fun, huh baby?"

"Of course. Did you come?"

"No"

"Are you hard?"

"Yes"

"Are you playing?"

"Yes"

"Mmm, nice. I want to come again before you go."

"Please do!"

"Mmm manage a trois. You in my pussy and him in my mouth. Now him in my pussy and you in my back door. Oooo manage a trois. Oh my gosh! Now you in my pussy and him in my mouth. Now him in my mouth and you in my back door. Oh my gosh! Oooo manage a trois! Aaaah! Oh, baby!"

She went on for a while longer, all the time the toy buzzing in the back ground. At last she asked "Did you come baby?"

"No, did you?"

"I did! A lot. Could you tell?"

"Yes, of course."

"You didn't get turned on?"

"Well, it's a turn on hearing you play and hearing you come. But it's a little weird hearing you talk about 'him' all the time. It makes me wonder if you have someone specific in mind."

"I don't have anyone special in mind. It's just a fantasy."

"That's cool"

"I guess I should let you go."

"No rush."

"But you're not enjoying the fantasy, and I want to indulge a bit more."

"OK" he said. He sort of wanted to come with her again, but she was so into her fantasy that he could not really get her involved in real phone sex. Which was cool. "Enjoy the fantasy, Chong-kyu."

"Thanks, baby! Good night." The sound of the toy started up again in the back ground.

"Good night, cutie pie." He said.

He still had a pretty good hard on. So he imagined having sex with Chong-kyu and a big breasted blond girl while he jacked-off. Then he fell sound asleep.

Change of Focus

The recliner was a bit more comfortable with only one person in it. But it was not nearly as fun. Cheryl had been sitting in his lap as they watched a mindless movie on DVD. Not that they had been paying much attention to the movie. Mostly they had been kissing and caressing each other absent mindedly.

Cheryl had stood up a few moments ago, and Al had given her a questioning look. She had just smiled and cocked her head to the side. She might have been going to use the bathroom, or get them each a glass of wine, but there was something in her look that said it was not just a glass of wine. Al wondered what she was doing.

What she was doing, was standing in front of the full length mirror in her bed room. She gathered her long hair and wound it into a bun. She preferred to wear it loose, and that was Al's preference as well. But she had a reason to put it up, and besides, she looked good with her hair up too. She briefly looked over the rest of her body, turning to look at the way her strong, shapely legs ran up to her nude, perfectly shaped derriere, the top of which disappeared under her white silk camisole. Turning back to face the mirror, she peeled off the camisole and looked at her breasts. She raised her arms above her head and looked again. She lowered them, raised them again, considered for a moment, and made a decision.

A moment later, Al noticed her stepping out of the bed room. He looked over and smiled. She had put on a pair of satin running shorts but was naked from the waist up. Al's smile broadened as he noticed the look in her eyes. She put her arms up above her head and started walking toward him. "It is time for you to do what you said you would do." She said in a playful, scolding voice.

"What's that?" Al asked expectantly.

Cheryl set one knee on the arm of the recliner, swung over and set her other knee on the other arm. She looked down at Al and said "You promised to pay more attention to my breasts."

Al smiled. "Ah, Chong-kyu, you are awesome!" he said as he ran his hands up her front and cupped her breasts.

"Mmmmm!" Chong-kyu moaned as she leaned forward.

Al put his left arm around her waist to steady her and began kissing her right breast while he massaged her left breast. Chong-kyu moaned again. She pulled his head against her chest. It was harder for him to kiss her breasts that way, but Al didn't mind. He was happy to see how much she enjoyed what he was doing. Al kept at it, kissing and massaging, and soon Chong-kyu was gasping and calling his name. He did not stop until, after many minutes, Chong-kyu bent her head down to his ear and whispered though her moaning "Al, baby, please take me to the bed."

He picked her up and carried her to the bed, kissing her all the while. He paused briefly to help her out of her shorts, and then began kissing again. He kissed the lower part of her stomach and her thighs. She hummed happily, but ran her fingers into his hair and pulled gently upward.

"You're supposed to kiss my breasts, baby!" she said playfully. "Down there is just fine!" She rolled on top of him and, as he began kissing her breasts again, unfastened his pants.

They scooted to the top of the bed so that Al's head was propped up on the pillows. She pressed her breasts into his face, and lowered herself down onto him. They both gasped slightly and began rocking their hips in rhythm. Al kissed and massaged Chong-kyu's breasts, running his free hand through her hair and then down her back to her shapely derriere. He gave it a gentle squeeze, and then ran his hand up her back so he could hug her as they made love.

"Oh, baby!" Chong-kyu called out as she shuddered. She pushed herself up so that she was riding him, and in complete control. She rocked her hips and threw her head back. Al's hands were on her hips. She reached down and pulled them back up to her breasts. She held them there as she bounced up and down on top of him. His hands on her breasts helped steady her as she rocked, bounced and rode her way to waves of orgasms. "Oh, Al, baby!" she cried. "Oooooh!"

She fell forward on top of him. He pressed his chest against hers and rolled over on top of her.

"Ooooh, Chong-kyu!" he whispered in her ear as he drove deep inside her. He kissed her face, ears and neck, ran his hands though her hair, and called her name again and again.

Chong-kyu held him tight with her arms, and wrapped her legs around him. She felt his hand slide down her side. Then she gasped as he placed two fingers against her clit and two on her back door. He pressed gently, and she moaned. He began to rub, and she went over the edge again.

After some time, Al slowed. He was still driving deep inside her, but more slowly now. Chong-Kyu regained her composure. Al kissed her face gently even as he drove deep inside her, giving her the feeling that he was kissing her on the inside. He looked deep into her eyes. "Chong-Kyu, you are so beautiful and so wonderful." He said breathlessly.

She tried to say something back, but he was moving faster again, and all that came out was a moan. She could feel his excitement building, and it carried her along with it. Soon he was making the long deep thrusts that signaled he was on the edge. He pressed and rubbed with his hand again, and Chong-Kyu closed her eyes, threw her head back and screamed. Through her ecstasy could hear him roaring as her came inside her.

They lay for a long time, hardly moving except to kiss each other. Al took Chong-Kyu's hand, raised it to his mouth and kissed her palm. He gazed into her eyes. He kissed her some more.

Eventually, he got out of bed to bring them some water. When he returned, as he set the glasses on the night stand, Chong-Kyu took him in her hand, pulled him closer, and gave him a long slow affectionate kiss. She took him out of her mouth, looked up at him, and said, "Al, baby, breasts…"

So he straddled her chest, and lay his erection between her breasts. She pushed her breasts together to hug him, and he rocked his hips back and forth. They smiled at each other and then went back to hugging and kissing.

Worth Waiting for It?

Al pushed the wet hair back from Cheryl's face. He looked in her eyes, smiled, and said "OK, it's time."

Cheryl smiled, giggled, and pulled him closer as the warm water from the shower ran over them. She squeezed his butt and said "I was beginning to think you were trying to avoid it." She said.

"No, I said I would. And I always keep my word. Especially when I tell you something. Ready?"

"I am!" she replied with a wicked grin. "How should I sit, or should I stand?"

"Either way…which ever seems more fun…maybe I can kiss better if you stand."

"OK," she said "I'll stand then." She turned, leaned forward against the wall of the shower, and spread her legs slightly.

Al kissed the back of her neck and then began kissing his way down her back.

"Al, baby, please don't tease. I'm too excited. I don't need kisses on my back."

"But I want to enjoy your whole body, especially your legs. If you're so excited, why not start playing with yourself. It might help…"

"I already am!" she laughed.

"Ah, Chong-kyu, you are awesome!" Al said. He kissed more quickly down to her waist. He paused for a moment to kiss each of her ass cheeks. Chong-kyu moaned with pleasure, and then moaned again in mild frustration when he began kissing his way down he shapely legs. "I can't resist your legs, baby." He said apologetically. But he put his hands back on her perfectly formed ass as he kissed his way back up. When he reached her lovely derriere, he began kneading with his hands and kissing.

Chong-kyu groaned with pleasure. He continued to knead her ass cheeks, but stopped kissing and began licking. "Oh, Al! Oh, baby!" she moaned. He pushed he cheeks apart and she felt the water from the shower run down between them. "Oh, baby, please!" she cried as she rubbed her pussy.

Al chuckled, squeezed her cheeks, and began licking her back door. "Oh, oh, oh, Al, oh…" was all she managed to say. Al kept at it, knowing she was having a grand time. From time to time he would back off to lick her ass cheeks quickly, but then went right back to licking her back door. "Oh, Al, baby, I'm going to come!" she called out. She began keening and shaking and shuddering. When her legs buckled he caught her and lowered her down onto the floor. He laid her on her back and positioned himself above her.

"Oh, Al!" she moaned happily as he slid into her warm pussy. She reached up and pulled his head down to kiss him. He hesitated but she just laughed and said "It's OK, baby, we're both clean, remember?" So he kissed her.

Soon she was riding another wave of orgasms. Al smiled and looked down at her. He reached his hand around and pressed his thumb on her back door. She groaned, and he pressed it part way in. "Oh, baby!" she gasped. He pressed it all the way into her back door. "Oh, baby!" she cried again, "I'm going to come!" and she did.

She caught her breath and said "Your turn for fun, baby!"

He looked puzzled. She pushed his hips back so he slid out of her pussy. She rolled her hips up, smiled and winked, and then guided him slowly into her back door.

"Oh, Chong-kyu, you are awesome!" he said. He began moving slowly in and out.

"Baby?"

"Yes?"

"Don't come in my ass, OK?"

"Uh, OK…"

"I want to see you come. It's fun!"

"Oh, OK" he laughed. He drove slowly in and out of her back door.

"Are you almost ready to come, baby?"

"Sure" he said. He knew she let him fuck her in the ass mostly for fun rather than pleasure, so he was happy to move to the next step…whatever it would be. He slid out of her back door.

"Here, lie back and relax, baby." She said as she slipped out from under him. She squeezed some shampoo onto her hand, grabbed his erection, and began pumping it. "Don't worry, baby, I'll kiss it too. I just want to make sure it's clean, and also, this is fun." She scooted down and began licking his balls as she pumped him.

Al groaned. "Wow" he said breathlessly.

Chong-kyu moved her hand to rub his balls as the water rinsed the shampoo away. Then she grabbed him with her right hand and began kissing him. With her left hand she began rubbing the area behind his balls. She pressed her head down to deep throat him.

"Oh, wow!" he gasped.

She lifted her head. "Ready to come, baby?"

He nodded.

She started stroking him again with her left hand. She started licking his balls again. She slid two fingers up his ass and began massaging his prostate.

"Wah!" he moaned incoherently.

She pumped faster. "Come on, baby, let me see it!" she said. She started licking his balls again, and pressed her fingers firmly against his prostate.

"Gaaaah!" he shouted and shot a huge load into the air.

She quickly climbed on top of him. Before he could even wonder what she was doing, she said "I want to come one more time, baby!" She began playing with herself and slid herself down so his erection slid back up her ass. "Oh, yeah!" she cheered. She rocked her hips and played with her pussy with great enthusiasm. "Oh, baby! Oh, Al! I'm going to come!" she cried, and she gushed onto his stomach.

"Oh, baby." She said breathlessly. "Oh, Al, baby." She said more softly. She lay down on top of him, feeling him pop out of her. She rested her head on his shoulder.

He stroked her hair. "Wow…" he said.

They lay together like that, letting the water wash them clean. They had a few fits of happy laughter. Finally, they got up, turned off the water, and dried each other. They walked arm in arm to the bed, climbed in, and held each other as they drifted off to sleep.

The Red Eye

Picking up people who had flown in on the Red Eye, the late night flight from LA that arrived on the East Coast in time for work in the morning, was one of the worst parts of being an intern. People getting off the Red Eye were generally a miserable, grumpy lot. But picking up people at the airport was one of the tasks given to interns, so Jimmy had to do it. He had been warned that Al was a little bit eccentric, but it did not worry him much. All he had to do was pick him up at Logan Airport in Boston, and bring him to the office. What Al did as he presented the results of the conference was Al's problem, not his.

No one had told him what Al looked like, or even his last name, and he had not thought to ask. So he just stood in the luggage area holding up a sign that read simply "AL". He was looking for someone dressed in a suit , or at least business casual, so he was a little surprised when a tall, thin man in a thread bare Army sweat shirt, sunglasses, and what looked like the pants from a track suit, ambled up to him and said "You must be my ride."

"Al?"

Al nodded.

"I guess we better get your luggage."

"This is all I have." Al said plainly, holding up a medium size gym bag.

"That's it?"

"If you roll a suit, shirt, and tie just right, they don't wrinkle."

"Ah...   ...OK...   ...this way then." Jimmy said, turning to walk to the car.

There was something odd about Al. It wasn't the clothes, people often dressed like hobos when traveling these days. It was not the sunglasses; they were standard attire for many people as well. It was not even the suit rolled up in the gym bag; he knew a few people who traveled light. It was not even the fact that he was whistling the theme song to a Japanese cartoon as they walked through the parking garage. What was it?

Finally, as he saw Al toss his gym bag carelessly into the back seat, it hit him. Al was relaxed and seemed to be in a jaunty mood. Unlike most people, who look like they have been put through a meat grinder after taking the Red Eye, Al seemed to be relaxed. He yawned occasionally, but other than that, he seemed fine. Even after a connection on the NYC-Boston shuttle, Al looked almost perfectly content. How?

As Jimmy started the car, Al slipped into the passenger seat, reclined the seat back as far as it would go, and put his feet up on the dash board. Jimmy looked over.

"What happened to your other sock?" Jimmy asked.

"Long story!" Al said with a big grin. Jimmy was hoping to hear more. But Al just put his hands behind his head, smiled contentedly, and looked out the windshield.

As they drove through Boston to the office, Al thought back over the flight. He had to keep his thoughts under control, however, as he would need to stand up and walk into the office in about ten minutes.

It had been a wild coincidence that Al had wound up at the same conference as Cheryl Pak. But once they found each other, they made sure that their luck continued. They were having so much fun together, that they went so far as to change their flights so they could be on the same flight back together. It meant taking the Red Eye and sitting in coach, all the way in the back of the plane. But they didn't mind.

Really, sitting in the back two seats, in coach, which would have been cramped if they were alone, was not so bad when they were together. They seemed to need less space when they were together. At first, they slept. Al leaned on the wall, Cheryl leaned on Al, and they slid into a peaceful, contented slumber. They had been up all night, most of the nights of the conference, making love, talking, making love, cuddling, and making love, so it was not hard to sleep on the plane.

After about two and a half hours, Cheryl woke up. She was thirsty. She got up, somewhat stiffly, stretched, got a drink of water, and washed up briefly. When she got back to the seat, she found Al standing and stretching. He smiled at her, kissed her, and went to get a drink of water as well.

When he returned, Cheryl leaned against him again, but they could not get back to sleep. After a couple of minutes, she looked up at him and asked "What are you thinking, my dear?"

"Just thinking about the week…"

"Like what?"

"You know what!"

"Tell me. I've forgotten."

Al laughed lightly. It had taken him a while, but he had finally figured out that when Cheryl said she forgot, it just mean that she wanted him to tell her again. So he leaned over and whispered some of the finer details of the last few nights into her ear.

"Mmmm" Cheryl hummed happily, and snuggled closer. "Now I remember. That was nice!"

"So, what are you thinking, my treasure?"

"About the same…"

Al gave her a gentle squeeze. "Tell me…"

"I don't like to tell. You tell me some more." She teased.

"Like what?"

"Tell me one of your fantasies!"

"You want to hear a fantasy?"

"Definitely!"

"How would you like to join the mile high club?"

"The what?"

Al explained.

Cheryl looked around. Everyone else on the flight was either asleep of watching a movie. "I think that is a great idea!" she said, putting her hand between his legs and giving him a squeeze.

"Ah, Chong-kyu, you are awesome!" Al whispered in her ear.

They got up, looked around, and seeing that they were unobserved, slipped into the bathroom in the very back, the one that had a little more room. As soon as the door was closed, they began hugging and kissing. The bathroom seemed almost spacious that way. Chong-kyu pressed against him, and could feel him stiffening. Al squeezed her perfect derriere and whispered in her ear "Should I step outside a moment so that you can get out of your panties?"

"No need" she whispered back.

"You have enough room?"

"I don't need any room, silly." She said, hiking up her sun dress. "I'm not wearing any panties."

"Oh, Chong-kyu, you are amazing!" he whispered back. He helped her scoot up onto the sink, and then bent down to kiss her.

"You don't have to do that, baby." She said playfully.

"But I want to!" Al said, kissing her thighs. "I want to be sure you have a climax."

"It's just for fun in here. I don't really need one." she said playfully.

"This is fun. And I really want to!" Al said, burying his face between her thighs.

Chong-kyu was in no position to argue, even if she had wanted to. She ran her hands into his hair and gasped. "Oh, baby!" The thrill of the situation added to the sensations, and soon Chong-kyu was keening and trying not to cry out in ecstasy. But Al kept at it for a long time.

He only stopped when there was a sharp wrap on the bathroom door. Chong-kyu caught her breath and said "Occupied!"

"Well, OK" said the stewardess "but other people may need to use the rest room soon."

Chong-kyu pulled Al up by his ears. She giggled and whispered "Now, baby! I want you!"

Al was as ready as she was. He entered her. They both took a deep breath and gazed into each other's eyes. Then they kissed as they made love. Soon Chong-kyu was shuddering again. She wrapped her legs around his hips. "Come on, baby, give it to me!" she urged.

But just then there was another sharp wrap on the door. "Hey, you two! The Chief Bursar is on her way back here. And she has no sense of humor about this stuff. Now get out of there, quick!"

Al slid out of her, and Chong-kyu looked at him and said "But, baby, you didn't come yet."

"No worries. I don't need to come every time. I got plenty over the last few days."

"Ooooh…" Chong-kyu said, and kissed him. She smoothed her skirt down as he pulled up his pants. They slipped out of the rest room, and got back to their seats before the Chief Bursar arrived.

Chong-kyu snuggled up against him and pulled a blanket over their laps. "That was fun." she said, "But I want to finish the job."

"Chong-kyu, you know it would make a mess."

She slipped her hand down his pants and started playing with him anyway. Al took a deep breath through his nose. "You shouldn't do that too much. I may have to run to the bathroom to avoid the mess."

"You don't like it?" she asked in a lilting voice.

"Of course I like it! I like it too much. And it could get messy."

"Hmm," Chong-kyu said, "I know! Take off one of your socks!"

"Chong-kyu, you are amazing!" Al said, slipping off a sock and handing it to her.

She draped the airline blanket over his lap, opened his pants, slipped the sock over him, and began stroking slowly. She looked at him with an angelic smile. He leaned forward and began kissing her so that he would not groan audibly.

It was not long before Chong-kyu's expertise yielded results. Al stiffened and held her tight. Chong-kyu was amazed at how long and hard he came. Afterwards, he panted as she cleaned up with the sock.

"What are we going to do with this?" she asked, holding the messy sock.

"Put it in an air sickness bag. I'll throw it away in a minute."

Chong-kyu laughed, pulled the air sickness bad from the seat back in front of her, and deposited the sock. She closed the top and handed it to Al. He took it back to the waste basket and dumped it.

Back at the seat, they snuggled up again. Al slipped his hand between her legs. "I'm all set, baby." Chong-kyu said.

"You want me to move my hand?"

"No, I kind of like it there. You just don't have to do anything, that's all."

Al kissed her, and they drifted off into a sound sleep that lasted the rest of the way to NY. At the airport they had a big hug before Cheryl caught her connection to DC, and Al caught his flight to Boston.

WAITING

Waiting was not something she enjoyed. The anticipation, coupled with a bit of boredom, was hard to take. The TV was not helping. Cheryl Pak changed the channel a few times, but still found nothing that could hold her interest. She stifled a yawn and shifted her body, trying hard not to move her left leg which was propped up on the back of the couch so Al could draw an elaborate dragon coiled around it.

Al looked up from his work. "Are you bored, my treasure?" he asked.

"Not really…" she answered vaguely.

"Would like me to stop?"

"No," she said, more definitely, "I want to see the dragon."

Al returned to his work.

Cheryl yawned.

Al looked over at her.

"Sorry" she said.

"No problem, why don't you read a book or something?"

"A book? I can't even pay attention to the TV!" she laughed.

"Just a thought…"

"Hmmm…   …what do you think I should do?" she asked playfully.

"What would you like to do?"

"I don't know. You tell me!" she said with one of her mischievous smiles.

Al looked at her and raised an eyebrow. "Well, you could play with yourself."

"You want me to play with myself?"

"I do."

"Hmmm, that sounds like fun! I think I will!" she said decidedly. She slipped her panties down, got her right leg out of them, leaving them dangling from her left thigh. She began rubbing herself slowly.

Al smiled at her. He returned to his work, but looked over at her repeatedly. The dragon took longer to draw that way, but the waiting was not so bad.

After

Cheryl let herself back into her apartment. She looked around. It was a mess, but she smiled anyway. She took a moment to savor the scene; the way it had become a mess was fun to contemplate.

Al had said he would help clean-up before they left for the train station. But Cheryl had declined the offer. She told him she did not want to waste any of their precious time together doing chores. She had been surprised and delighted to see how happy he was to hear it.

"Are chores really that bad?" she had teased.

"No," he had replied "but the other things we can do with the time *are* that good."

So they had spent the last hour in the apartment making love. Ordinarily, after making love, she would lie on top of him and he would run his hand up and down her back and tell her how wonderful she was. But they had not had time. So she had leaned on him as he drove to the train station. And he had told her how wonderful she was then. It had been sweet in its own way. She smiled again thinking of it.

She took a deep breath and let it out slowly. Then she looked around the room. It was still a mess. She would have to clean it up. Then she could think more about the extended weekend she and Al had shared. Step one: clear away the wreckage of the Chinese take-out dinner from the night before.

Clean-up from dinner the night before was easy enough. Everything went in the trash, including the disposable chop sticks, and the trash bag went down the trash chute. Then the coffee cups; there was a pair of them on the night stand, a pair on the table in the living room, and another pair in the kitchen. They went into the dish washer, along with the whiskey glasses. She could tell her glasses from his because there was a bit of melted ice in the bottom of hers; Al took his whiskey straight.

Laundry next…there was not a lot of it, but what there was, was scattered all over the apartment. She gathered up stray bits of lingerie and other garments, finding some in the oddest places. She counted five pairs of panties. How had she gone through five pairs of panties in four days? Most of the time she hadn't been wearing any! No matter. She scooped them all up and put them in the basket. She also found a pair of his under pants. They went in the trash; there wasn't much left of them, she had torn them to shreds in a fit of playfulness.

She went to change the sheets on the bed. But as she bent over them, she could smell the scent of the weekend. Again, she smiled, and decided to change them later.

In the bathroom she gathered up towels and tossed them into the laundry basket. Then she spotted the cosmetics case on the counter. What the heck was she going to do with all the cosmetics? She never wore make-up. It was one of the things Al really liked about her. But, there it was. She'd have to find a place to store it until next time. Still, as she thought of the reason she had bought it, she smiled. She unfastened her pants and slid them down a bit. She smiled more broadly at the cartoon of the kitty cat nestled just above the adorable little patch of glossy black silk (as Al called it). The kitty cat was looking content and had a speech balloon that whispered *"Chong-kyuuuu"*, compete with little hearts. Al had even written it backwards so she could see it in the mirror. It made her laugh, but also made her miss him. It was his kind of thing.

He had drawn it as an experiment. They had planned for him to draw elaborate pictures on her body, and the kitty was a test to see how well the water based markers would wash off.

The marker did not wash off easily. So drawing a great dragon coiled around her leg was not a good idea. But Cheryl was not willing to give up, and she had an inspiration. "Let's go to the drug store." She had said suddenly, without explanation. Al didn't know what she had in mind, but her general mischievous nature, and spontaneity, promised great things. So he had readily agreed.

Cheryl had bought a large, prepackaged cosmetics kit, and a jar of cold cream. They had brought it back to the apartment, and had hours of fun creating art work on her body. Some cold cream and a hot shower were all that was needed to remove the art work. All except for the kitty cat. She had had him go over it in permanent marker so she could enjoy it for a few more days. The make-up went into the cabinet below the sink. She kissed the jar of cold cream. "Great facilitator" she thought as she put it in the medicine cabinet.

Some photos of the artwork, along with some sketches he'd done of her, hung on the walls. She would enjoy them too for a few more days, before taking them down.

Cheryl returned to the bed and sat down. She should change the sheets. "Later" she thought. She could still smell his body in them, and it was nice. She slipped out of her jeans and lay back on the bed. She missed him already. And she knew he missed her as well. She slipped out of her panties and looked down at the kitty cat whispering her Korean name. She could almost hear Al's voice in her ear whispering "Chong-kyuuuu". She smiled to herself as she ran her hands up and down her thighs and then up between her legs.

Cheryl Sends a Video

They had planned a long, sexy, fun phone conversation for the coming weekend. But then her job intervened. She had a sales conference and a dinner with clients. She had no idea when the dinner would end. And she knew Al would be disappointed. She didn't want to disappoint him, but what could she do? How could she make it up to him? How could she make him smile?

She could move the call up. But when she called, he didn't answer. Eventually, she got a text back from him. It read:

Sorry, baby cakes, working super late at the factory. Can I call you around 11PM?

Will be asleep by then. Something came up this weekend with work. Wanted to do the call tonight. Sorry.

Hmmm, wish we could talk. Was looking forward to it. Dang!

Cheryl looked at the text and thought for a moment. Then she typed:

Hey, baby, why don't you look at my picture tonight and play? Send me a text and tell me how much fun it was.

OK…If you will do it too.

OK, baby, have fun, and let me know.

Then she had a fun idea and added:

I will let you know too. And I won't disappoint!

OK

Cheryl put away her phone. She went to take a long shower and prepare. It would be a fun evening for both of them, even if it didn't happen at the same time.

After the shower she put on her white silk camisole and some lace panties. She retrieved the web cam from her dresser. She set her phone on a chair at the foot of her bed, plugged in the web cam, and checked the camera angle by taking a couple of selfies. She smiled to think of how much Al was going to like what she had in mind. Starting the video record, she leaned forward "Hi, Al baby, it's me, Cheryl. But by the end of this video, I think you'll be calling me Chong-kyu." She said playfully.

X   X   X   X

Al stumbled into his apartment. It was just as well that Cheryl could not take a call at 11PM, it was 12:45 now and he was totally beat. Though he would have liked to talk with her anyway, it was best to save their adventures for times they could both enjoy them.

He tossed his clothes into the basket and went to take a shower. As he was drying himself afterward, he picked up his phone to set his alarm. He found a text from Cheryl. It read:

Open your email, baby. Use code 2598492. You'll be glad you did! ☺

Al smiled and started his computer. Sure enough, there was an email from Cheryl with and encrypted attachment. He used the code to unlock it. It was a video. Good thing he had not bothered putting on his pajama pants he thought with a laugh. He stated the video.

Cheryl was sitting on the edge of her bed. It was really just a mattress and box spring on the floor. She was leaning on the knees of her beautiful legs. She smiled and said "Hi, Al baby, it's me, Cheryl. But by the end of this video, I think you'll be calling me Chong-kyu."

Al smiled, shook his head, and muttered "Oh, Chong-kyu, you are awesome."

Chong-kyu slid back on the bed. She slipped out of her panties and slowly spread her legs. "How do you like my latest wax job, baby?" she asked playfully. She ran her hands up and down her the inside of her thighs, smiling and winking at the camera.

Al felt the start of an erection coming on. He gazed at the screen and smiled.

"Hey, baby, are you playing yet? It's not nice to keep a lady waiting!" Cheryl teased.

She had a point. He wrapped his left hand around his member and started stroking slowly while he rubbed his balls with his right hand.

"Are you playing now, Al?" she asked. "Are you nice and hard? Maybe this will help." She added, lifting her camisole to show her lovely breasts. She squeezed them gently and pinched her nipples slowly. She winked at the camera, slowly running her right hand down her stomach and began slowly rubbing her pussy. With her left hand she continued playing with her breasts.

"Oh, Chong-kyu, you are so awesome!" Al murmured as he slowly pumped his erection.

"Are you calling me Chong-kyu yet?" she asked playfully. "I like when you call me that! It means you're excited. Are you excited, baby?"

Al nodded. He stopped rubbing his balls and used both hands to stroke his now super hard erection.

"Hey, baby, just thinking of you calling me Chong-kyu makes me feel hot. Want to see something crazy?" she asked. Before Al could even nod, she rocked her hips forward, and slid her right hand down her stomach. She slipped two fingers of her right hand into her sweet pussy, and began working her clit with two fingers of her left hand.

Al was pumping harder now. He actually slowed down to try to calm down. He was so excited by watching Chong-kyu play that he was on the verge of coming, and he wanted to wait until the end of the video. He stopped pumping for a moment and took several deep breaths.

Chong-kyu was really enjoying herself on the video. "Oh, baby, oh, Al, oh…oh my gosh!!" she gasped and shuddered. "Al, baby, are you still playing? Did you come?" she asked, still rubbing her pussy.

Al continued to stroke slowly. He knew there was more in store, and he didn't want to come until the end. "Chong-kyu…you are amazing…" he murmured again.

"Are you still playing? I want to come one more time, but I want you to come with me. So I'm going to do something I know will make you come. But I want you to pause the video, and play until you are about to come. Then you can start it again and we can come together. Ready? Here goes…!"

Al stroked slowly, he was near the edge anyway.

Chong-kyu continued rubbing her pussy with her right hand. She rolled onto her side. She ran her left hand over her shapely ass, squeezing and massaging her beautiful ass cheeks.

Al continued stroking and smiled. He knew what was next.

Sure enough, Chong-kyu slid her hand between her cheeks. Still rubbing her pussy with her right hand, she took the middle finger and ring finger of her left hand and pressed them into her back door. "Oooh, Al, baby, do you like it? Mmmm, fuck me in the ass! Do you like fucking me in the ass?" she worked her pussy harder and faster with her right hand, and plunged her fingers deeper into her back door. "Oh, baby! Oh, Al, baby! I'm going to come baby! Come on, baby, come with me. Oh, my gosh!" she gasped and shuddered.

Al shuddered too. "Ahhh!" he groaned as he shot a huge messy load all over the sheets. "Oh, wow…" he sighed as he squeezed the last of the load out. He didn't care about the mess on the sheets. He was breathing hard and chuckling to himself about the amazing show Chong-kyu had put on for him. He looked at the screen again. Chong-kyu was smiling at the camera and breathing hard too. She lifted her legs to give him one more look at her rubbing her pussy and back door. Then she slipped her left hand away from her back door, but continued rubbing her pussy. "Did you come, baby? I bet you did! But I'll call later just to be sure. Love you!" still rubbing her pussy, she turned off the camera.

"Love you too, Chong-kyu, my crazy lady." Al whispered. He turned off his PC. He cleaned up the mess on the sheets as best as he could with his t-shirt. He threw the old t-shirt in the laundry. He put on a fresh t-shirt but did not bother with under pants. He turned off the light, climbed into bed, and drifted off to sleep thinking happy thoughts about Chong-kyu Pak.

X   X   X   X

His phone was ringing. Al fumbled on his night stand, picked up the phone, and was about the send it to voice mail when he saw the caller ID. It read "CK Pak". He tap the answer button. "Hello, beautiful." He said in a sleepy but happy mumble.

"Hey, Al, did you come?"

"Of course!"

"Did you call me Chong-kyu?"

"Naturally"

"Did you pause it like I asked you to so we could come together?"

"There was no need."

"Nice! So you came with me?"

"Oh, yes!"

"Do you want to come again?"

"Now?"

"Sure, why not?" she said.

Al could hear her vibrator turn on. "Oh, Chong-kyu, you are awesome!" he said as he reached down, wrapped his hand around his stiffening member and began stroking.

A Memory and a Morning

Al rolled over a couple of times, first on one side, then on the other. But it was no use. He was waking up. He had slept somewhat fitfully. He had a lot on his mind. But, unlike most people who toss and turn, it was a riot of happy thoughts ricocheting around in his brain that made him sleep so lightly.

Well, if he was going to wake up, there was no point in fighting it. He opened his eyes, stretched, rolled out of bed, and staggered over to the bathroom. As long as he was there, he took the time to brush his teeth, and shave. It would make waking up in the morning more pleasant. He was not sure what time it was, and he did not really care. It was dark out. So he would get back into bed.

He leaned back against the big hotel pillows and looked over at Cheryl. Her long black hair was splayed out over one of the pillows. Most of her back was exposed, her beautiful golden skin stood out against the stark white of the linen hotel sheets. Al gazed at her and smiled. It was great to be with her after so long. They met sporadically, and due to their crazy schedules, they had not seen each other in over a year. But now, now they had some real time together. No need to rush.

Al rolled onto his back and gazed at the ceiling. It had been quite a reunion. Cheryl was quite a lady. Sometimes when they got together they had wild sex. Sometimes they made sweet love. Often, as was the case this time, they did both.

Cheryl was so much fun when she was feeling playful that he sometimes forgot how sweet she could be when she was feeling romantic. Last night they had held each other for a long time before drifting off to sleep. He closed his eyes and took a long breath through his nose as he thought about it. The love making had been slow and unhurried. It had been simple and wonderful. No crazy changing positions every few minutes. Just intense intimacy. The thing he remembered most about it was the way Cheryl had held him so tight the whole time.

He glanced over at her again. Such and amazing lady. So sweet, and yet able to be a bit crazy too. Before the long leisurely lovemaking, they had gone to dinner so that he could recover his energy. Because before dinner, she had wanted a bit of craziness. It had actually started a week earlier while they were talking on the phone, making final plans for the weekend.

"Hey, baby," she had said, toward the end of the conversation, "can you do me a favor?"

"Sure, what?"

"Don't masturbate for a week."

"What?"

"Don't masturbate for a week. Can you do that for me?"

"Ah, sure…"

"And I want you to look at plenty of internet porn. OK?"

"Ah…OK…"

"You can play a bit, but don't come. OK?"

"Ah, OK, I guess you want me to conserve my strength. Which is fine, but I'll be on a hair trigger by the time I get to your hotel. The first time won't last very long if I do all of that."

"That's OK! I want to watch you come. And I want a big messy show. So, can you do that for me?"

"If that's what you want. But it seems like kind of a waste…"

"No, I won't ask you to jerk-off. I'll take care of you. I just want a good show. Fair?"

"Sure, OK."

"You're a sweetie!"

"So are you!"

They had wrapped up the phone call with Al asking Cheryl to think of him and play with herself that night, which she agreed to do. Al had, as requested, viewed some internet porn, but refrained from jacking off.

He had spent some time each night watching videos of beautiful Asian women having wild sex with men, with groups of men, with women, and with groups of women. And though he had given himself a few strokes, he had not come. During the five hour drive to their rendezvous he had thought about all the wild sex they had had over the years. By the time he arrived at her hotel he felt about ready to explode.

They'd had a quick glass of wine at the hotel bar and then gone right upstairs to her room. Cheryl had turned to him as soon as the door was closed and said "The bathroom is over there. You can get cleaned up, and then make yourself comfortable on the couch."

"Should I take off my pants?"

"If you like. I'm just going to slip into something more comfortable and I'll be right out." Cheryl said as she stepped into the bed room, closing the door behind her.

A minute or so later, Al sat on the couch in just his sweat shirt. His pants were draped over the chair in the corner. Cheryl emerged from the bed room dressed only in a black French cut T-shirt. She wore it not to cover her breasts, she had beautiful breasts, but because for some reason Al found the top only look tremendously exciting, and she wanted him as excited as possible. "Ready, baby?" she asked.

"Ready" he answered with a smile and an erection that showed he was telling the truth.

Cheryl knelt between his legs, held the base of his erection in her right hand, started rubbing his balls with her left, and brought her mouth down on him. Al gasped. He had almost forgotten how incredibly well Cheryl did that.

"Tell me when you're ready to come, OK?"

Al just nodded, trying not to lose it right then. He managed to get control of himself so that he could enjoy Cheryl's amazing blow job for at least a minute or two. But it wasn't easy. Cheryl was using all of her considerable skill and boundless enthusiasm; sucking him, pumping him, licking his balls, sucking some more. All Al could do was groan.

"Ready to come now, baby?" Cheryl asked.

"Uh huh!" Al grunted.

Cheryl smiled with her usual joyous enthusiasm and began pumping him as fast as she could. "Come on, baby, give it to me!" she said and opened her mouth wide. "Come on, baby!" she urged him as she pumped and played with his balls. She opened her moth wide again, aiming him as best she could as she pumped.

That was all it took. Al's body jerked and convulsed as he shot a huge load. Most went into her mouth, but some hit her cheek, some landed on her chin, some got on her shirt, and a few drops even landed on her thighs. She started laughing, then she started coughing. She steadied herself by putting her hands on the floor. She stopped coughing, gulped and looked up at him. "Wow, I was afraid I was going to have to spit it out!"

"You swallowed it?"

"Of course! Well, as much as I could. Some of it didn't go in my mouth so…"

Al laughed "Oh, Chong-kyu, you are incredible." He said appreciatively.

"Not too crazy?"

"No, just the right amount of crazy. And a very good kind of crazy. Just fabulous."

Cheryl smiled at him. Then she said "Hey, baby, you're still pretty hard. Mind if I ride you for a bit?"

"Please do!"

Cheryl stood up, put her knees on the couch, positioned him, and lowered herself down onto him. "Mmmm, nice!" she said.

"Oh, wow!" Al sighed. He kissed her forehead.

"Want to lick the come off my face?" She asked.

"Ah, not really."

"French Kiss?"

"Sure" he said with a chuckle.

They sat like that for a long while, hugging, kissing, Cheryl grinding her hips. At last Al said "Hey, honey, I don't think I'm hard anymore. Sorry I didn't make you come."

"That's OK!" she said brightly. "That wasn't the point this time. I just wanted to see you come. Riding you was a little bonus. Besides, we have plenty of time. And I know you'll make me come later. You always do."

After that they had washed up and gone down to dinner, returning right after to make sweet love.

Thinking about the crazy blow job now made Al laugh to himself.

"Oh," Cheryl said, "are you awake?"

"Yup"

"What's so funny?"

"Just thinking about last night."

"Nice! Which part."

"Well, at first I was thinking about how we made love late into the night. That part made me smile. Then I thought about the blow job. That made me laugh."

"Really? It just made you laugh? It didn't make you excited?"

"Well," Al said "Let me put it this way." He rolled over and pressed his erection against Cheryl's thigh.

"Oh, nice! Is that for me?"

"Of course!" He said kissing her.

"Come here, baby!" she said, lying on her back.

Al rolled on top of her and tried to enter her, but she was not quite ready. Al kissed her on the fore head, on the mouth, and on her neck. He kissed down her chest, Cheryl moaned softly and smiled as he kissed each of her beautiful breasts. He kissed his way down her stomach and then began kissing her thighs. He kissed down as far as her knees. Cheryl spread her legs and he began kissing the insides of her thighs, working his way upward again. "Oh, Chong-kyu, you have such a pretty pussy." He said softly.

"Mmm, thanks, baby." She answered softly as well.

Then they said nothing because Al buried his face between her legs and began kissing with joyous enthusiasm. Chong-kyu ran her hands though his hair, arched her back and moaned softly. Al kept kissing, enjoying every moment and everything about her body. After a time Chong-kyu shuddered briefly and she gasped "Oh, my gosh!" Al kept kissing. Chong-kyu began rocking her hips. Al kept kissing. "Oh, my gosh!" she gasped again. Al kept kissing. Finally, her body shook, she cried out, and her thighs came together. She reached down and grabbed his shoulders, pulling gently upward.

Al slid up onto her, and guided himself into her. She put her arms around him and pulled him close. The warmth of her body, the sound of her moans of pleasure, the smell of her hair, the feel of her golden skin, and the feeling of sliding all the way into her, so that the end of his erection was kissing the deepest part of her pussy filled his senses. Nothing else mattered for a long time. He turned his head slightly to kiss her ear. She was so pretty. He wanted to see her. Slowly he pushed himself up so he could look down at her. She was so lovely. He gazed at her golden skin, her beautiful breasts, and her lovely face; turned slightly to the side, eyes closed, mouth open slightly, moaning softly…so very wonderful.

Chong-kyu grasped the back of his arms, pulling him gently downward. He lowered himself back down and she wrapped her arms around him again. He reached down and rubbed her smooth and supple derriere. He pressed two fingers on her back door.

"I'll come when you come, baby." Chong-kyu said softly.

"Don't you want to come now and again later?"

"I want to come when you come. I always do."

"OK" he said, not knowing what else to say. He kissed her face a few times and began rubbing her derriere again. Chong-kyu moaned some more. Al stopped thinking and just rocked his hips in time with hers. He drove gently but firmly deep inside her, kissing the deepest part of her pussy with his erection. He could feel her pussy ballooning and he could feel the pressure building inside him. He let the feeling carry him away, and Chong-kyu did the same. Soon they were both howling and shuddering as they came together. Al lay on top of her, breathing hard. They held each other tight for a long time. Finally, Chong-kyu relaxed her grip and he rolled off of her. They lay side by side, embracing and kissing gently for a long time.

The grey light of dawn was coming through the windows when they finally decided to go down stairs and get some breakfast. Usually when they ate together, they chatted quite a bit. But this morning they just gazed at each other and smiled.

A Memory and a Morning Part 2

After breakfast they went back up to the room to make love again. They didn't talk, they didn't need to. They just got undressed and climbed back into bed, hugging and kissing. Al smiled at Cheryl, who smiled back. He kissed her on the nose and then began kissing his way down her body. He paused at her breasts. She moaned happily as he took his time there, kissing and sucking and gently massaging. He was usually so excited about kissing her lovely pussy that he rushed past her lovely breasts. But he had plenty of time, and they were feeling relaxed, so he took his time. Cheryl had almost forgotten how good it could feel to have her breasts kissed. Now she remembered. Pleasure and excitement flowed through her body. She held his head against her chest, giving him just enough leeway to kiss.

"Oh, baby!" she moaned, "Oh, honey! Oh…oh my gosh!" she cried as her body shuddered. She pulled Al back up so she could kiss his face. As they kissed, she gasped his hand and guided it down between her legs. Al began rubbing, and Cheryl moaned happily. They shared several long slow French kisses. Cheryl moaned through them. Then she pulled back a little to say "Al, baby, kiss."

"Kiss?"

"Down there, baby."

Al smiled. He kissed his way back down to her pussy. It was such a pretty pussy, and such fun to kiss. Cheryl purred and ran her hands though his hair as he kissed. When she began to writhe, Al slipped his hands under her derriere so that he could massage her cheeks as he kissed her pussy. "Oh my gosh!" Cheryl cried softly. Al kept kissing. "Oh, baby!' she cried again.

Al kept kissing. "Oh! Oh, oh, oh!" she cried, and Al had to stop kissing because she brought her legs together and rolled on her side. "Oh, baby, I want you. Are you ready?"

"Not quite yet. My mind is ready, but my body hasn't caught up. Sorry."

"That's OK. We can rest a bit, or go for a walk or something."

"Should I kiss you some more?"

"Ah, I don't know…"

"I'd like to…I want to make you gush."

"You're too silly."

"You don't want to gush for me?"

"I do! But I'm not sure just kissing will do it. Sometimes it does, but not every time."

"It's worth a try."

"Hmm, I think you're right. But there is one way to be sure I gush."

"Yeah?"

Cheryl raised her legs above her head, spreading them wide. "Lick my ass while I play!" she said playfully.

"Oh, Chong-kyu, you are awesome!" Al said. He set to work licking and massaging Chong-kyu's shapely ass. She slid her hand down her stomach, gave Al a mischievous wink, and began rubbing her pussy.

"Wow, so sexy" Al said, "So hot!" and resumed licking and massaging.

Chong-kyu slipped two fingers into her pussy and began working her G-spot.

"So sexy…so sweet!" Al murmured as he licked her derriere.

"Ooooh!" Chong-kyu moaned "Oh! Oh, baby…Oh, baby! Oh, honey…I think I'm going to come! Oh baby, I think I'm going to gush! OH, baby, I'M GOING TO GUSH!" And she did.

Chong-kyu brought her legs back down, grabbed Al by the shoulders and pulled.

Al slid up over her. He kissed her face. "Chong-kyu, you are awesome!" he whispered.

Chong-kyu grasped his face between her palms. "Let me taste…" she said with a grin, and licked his face.

"Nice?"

"Mmmm, but now I want to watch you play…"

"I don't know…it seems like a waste."

"But I feel funny if I come without you…"

"Well, we can come together…" he said, pressing his now hard erection against her thigh.

"Nice!" she said, guiding him into her. "Mmm, so nice."

Al began sliding in and out, and Chong-kyu purred. She looked up at him. "Al, baby, why don't you want to play for me?"

"Oh, I think it would be fun. It just seems like a waste to do it now."

"When?"

"How about right before I leave? Then it won't be a waste. And it will give us something to laugh about as we each drive home."

"Nice!" Chong-kyu said with a smile. Then she began rocking her hips in a most wonderful way. They did not talk anymore for a while. They just made love that was at once sweet and great fun.

After spending most of the day on hiking trails, they made their way back to the hotel. Cheryl would spend the night at the hotel, but Al had to drive through the night to get home in time to take care of some work around the house and get ready for work the next day.

Back in the room, Al stuffed his things into his duffle bag while Cheryl checked her messages. He carried his duffle bag to the door and turned to give Cheryl one more hug and kiss before leaving. He started and then smiled. Cheryl was standing in the middle of the room. She was wearing a light blue T-shirt that highlighted the golden color of her skin. She wore nothing else.

"Do you think we have time to make love once more?" he asked hopefully.

"Nice try, baby!" she said with a naughty smile "Did you forget? You were going to jack-off for me."

"Oh…yeah…"

"Come on, you promised…" she said playfully.

"I didn't promise, but I said I would, so…OK" Al said, unfastening his pants. He slid his pants down and stepped out of them. He was already starting to get hard as he stood up. "Where should I stand?" he asked as he began pumping.

Cheryl walked over to the chair in the corner and sat down. "Come stand over here. Let me see from a couple different angles."

Al walked over, pumping, and stood in front of her. "How is this, Chong-kyu, my sweet?" he asked turning sideways to her so she could see his hand going up and down on his erection.

"Nice!" Chong-kyu replied. "Now turn the other way. Nice! Now let me see from the front. Nice! Can you do it two handed?"

Al demonstrated that he could. "What next?" he asked.

"Just do whatever is most fun for you. I'll just enjoy the show."

Al resumed the one handed stroke, turning to one side from time to time so she could see him stroking the length of his erection, and then back toward her so that he was aiming right at her again. After a minute or so he began looking around.

"What are you looking for, baby?" Chong-kyu asked.

"Kleenex"

"You don't need Kleenex, silly."

"I will soon."

"No, silly!" she said raising her shirt. "Just come on my chest!"

"Oh, Chong-kyu, you are awesome!" he said.

"I know." Chong-kyu said.

Al stepped forward so that his erection was over Chong-kyu's lovely breasts as he pumped faster and faster. "Oh, baby, ready?" he asked tightly.

"Give it to me, baby!"

"Oh, baby, I'm going to come! I'm going to come! Oh, baby, I'm coming! I'm coming!" he gasped as he popped his rocks onto Chong-kyu's left breast. He scooted over and squeezed out a little more onto her right breast. "Aaah, wow…" he sighed.

"Fun?" Chong-kyu asked.

He nodded. "I guess I better get some Kleenex now." He added.

"Oh, non-sense!" Chong-kyu said. "I can clean that up. No trouble." She grasped the base of his erection and pulled him forward, taking him in her mouth and giving him an appreciative suck.

"Wow! He said.

"Mmm" she moaned.

"Do you need Kleenex for your chest?" he asked after she had finished sucking.

"Nope!" she said with a wink and just pulled her shirt back down. "I kind of like the feeling. I can take a shower later I guess."

Al just chuckled appreciatively.

They got dressed. Chong-kyu put on a sweat shirt even though it was warm outside. The come shot had soaked through her T-shirt.

In the parking lot they had a long hug.

"I love you, baby." Chong-kyu said.

"I love you too." Al replied.

One more kiss, one more hug, and then Al got into his car and drove off. Cheryl went back to the room. She took a quick shower, but resolved to call Al the next day. She was not sure what they would talk about, but she would think of something.

Cheryl Pak's Birthday

Al was packing for a visit with Cheryl Pak. He had a twelve pack of condoms, a fresh bottle of lube, tooth brush, shaving kit, and a change of clothes. Was there anything else he needed? For some reason he thought he did, but he didn't know what it was. As he pondered, his phone rang.

He picked it up, and checked the screen. It was a call from Cheryl. Best of all, it was a video call.

"Hello, my treasure." He said as he pushed the answer button and saw Cheryl's beautiful face.

"Hello, my dear, are you ready for the weekend?"

"Of course. I'm just finishing my packing. I'll leave at the crack of dawn. I should be at the hotel by late morning."

"Nice!"

"I was thinking…is there anything in particular you want me to bring?"

"No, nothing in particular. But it is going to be my birthday, and I have some ideas about how we can celebrate."

"Really? What did you have in mind?"

"You'll have to wait and find out. But I will tell you this: I have four cards here, one for each type of fun." Cheryl said, holding up four playing cards. "Depending on my mood at any given time, I will use one of the cards, and you have to play along. Fair?"

"Sure" Al said with a laugh. He knew it would be fun.

"OK, see you soon, sweetie!"

"OK, see you then." Al said. Cheryl hung up. Crazy Lady! He thought appreciatively. Then he checked his watch. He has just about enough time to get to the video store before it closed. He didn't need a video, but they sold other things there as well.

XXX

In the hotel room they had a long hug. "Happy Birthday, Cheryl my treasure." Al said.

"Thanks, baby. Ready for fun?"

"Absolutely! But don't you want your present first?"

"You got me a present?"

"Naturally"

"Nice! What is it?"

Al stepped back. He reached into his travel bag and pulled out a package about the size of dictionary wrapped in colorful paper. He handed it to Cheryl.

She held it for a moment, looked up, and smiled.

"Open it!" Al urged.

Cheryl peeled the tape back carefully at first, then she just shrugged and tore the paper away. Inside was a polished wooden box. She set it on the table and lifted the cover. Inside, nestled in velvet like a set of dueling pistols, was a pair vibrators. One was gold, the other silver. Cheryl looked up at Al, smiled mischievously, and raised an eyebrow. "I hope you have some plans for helping me enjoy my present." She said.

"Oh. Yes…"

"Nice…and here are the birthday cards." Cheryl said, holding up four playing cards. She laid them down on the table explaining each one. "The

Queen of Hearts means I want to be romantic, obviously. The Queen of Diamonds means I want to do something sweet and fun. The Queen of Spades means I want to do something really naughty, and I want to be in charge. And, finally, the Queen of Clubs means I want to do something naughty, and I want you to be in charge."

"Well, Chong-kyu, my treasure, it's your birthday. So, as the magicians say, pick a card, any card."

The Queen of Hearts

Chong-kyu set the Queen of Hearts down on the table. She pulled up some romantic music on her i-phone and gave Al a sweet smile.

Al stood up, walked over to Chong-kyu and held out his arms. She rose and stepped into them. They slow danced through a few songs, they had a few long slow French kisses. He picked her up and carried her to the bed room. He layed her gently on the bed and began kissing her face. She kissed back and cooed with pleasure. Al slid her T-shirt up and out of the way. Chong-kyu was not wearing a bra. "beautiful..." Al murmured. He bent down and began kissing Chong-kyu's lovely breasts. She moaned happily, running her hands through his hair.

Chong-kyu felt warmth and pleasure flow through her body. "Oh, honey, oh that's so nice..." she moaned happily. Al kept kissing, first one breast then the other. Chong-kyu pulled his face back up to hers and they had a long slow French kiss. He massaged her beautiful breasts with one hand and squeezed her shapely ass with his other. Chong-kyu moaned, and Al began kissing her neck and ears. They rolled over, and Al began running his hands up and down her back, tracing her spine and rubbing her perfectly shaped ass each time his hands arrived there. They rolled again so that Al was on top. Chong-kyu reached down and guided him into her. They both sighed as he slipped inside. Her pussy was so warm and wet. Al kissed her face and looked into her eyes. "I love you, Chong-kyu" he said softly to her.

"I love you too, Al." she said. She felt him getting harder just from hearing her say that. It made her smile. Then she closed her eyes and just concentrated on the warm pleasure flowing through her body as Al drove gently deep inside her, kissing the deepest part of her pussy with his erection. He stroked her hair and kissed her face as they ground their hips together.

"Oh, Chong-kyu, you are so wonderful..." he murmured into her ear. He reached down to massage her derriere as they made love. Chong-kyu moaned happily.

They made love for a long time. Al wanted her to come, so he placed his little finger and ring finger on her clit and his index and middle finger on her back door. He started rubbing.

"Mmmm, nice." Chong-kyu said. "Oh, baby, that's so nice."

They had another long French kiss. Then Chong-kyu said "I'll come when you come."

"You can come now, and when I come..."

"I just want to come together. It seems sweeter."

"As you wish, my treasure."

"Are you ready?"

"Pretty close...ready for a grand finale?"

"Mmm, I am! I'll come when you come, I'm ready any time."

"Oh, Chong-kyu, you are so awesome..." He said, and kissed her again. He began moving his hips faster, and Chong-kyu felt the waves building inside her.

"Oh, baby, oh, my gosh!" she said. She wrapped her legs around his hips and squeezed his shoulders with all her might. She could feel him breathing faster and his erection getting harder and bigger. "Oh, baby..." she said, and then just let out a series of long groans as the feeling built more and more and her pussy began ballooning. She felt his body convulse and heard him roaring as he came inside her with a long shuddering orgasm. She let the feeling carry her away, and let out a long howl of ecstasy as she shuddered with a series of strong and wonderful orgasms.

They kept moving for a while, but more slowly. Eventually they slowed to a stop. They had another French kiss. Their mouths were dry from moaning and groaning. Al slipped out of her. He kissed his way down her sweat slicked stomach to her pussy. He gave it an affectionate kiss. Then he went and got them a couple of glasses of water. When he returned, Chong-kyu reached out, grasped his still semi hard member, and guided him forward so she could give it a few appreciative sucks. Al stroked her hair as she did it. When she let him go he slid into bed beside her and wrapped her in his arms. They held each other for a long time, had one more kiss, and drifted off to sleep.

"Ah, some crazy fun…what did you have in mind my treasure?"

"Oh…I thought we might do an around the world…"

"Ah, Chong-kyu, you are awesome!"

"I know!" she said, slipping her panties off and tossing them to him.

"What do I do with these?" Al asked.

"I don't know…maybe we'll think of something" Chong-kyu said. She began rubbing her pussy.

"Oh, Chong-kyu, it's so sweet when you do that…"

"Just sweet? Not sexy?"

"Sweet and sexy…you know I think it's pretty."

"Pretty?"

"Of course, it's always pretty when you feel good. And sexy too."

"How sexy?" she asked playfully.

"This sexy!" Al replied, holding his hands out wide.

"Don't show me that way, silly! Show me the real way."

Al smiled. He reached down and wrapped his hand around his stiffening member. "This sexy!" he said as he began to pump.

"Oooh, nice!" Chong-kyu said appreciatively.

They watched each other play for a bit. Then Al knelt down beside the bed and began kissing Chong-kyu's thighs. "So pretty…" he murmured between kisses.

"You like watching me play, baby?"

"You know I do!" Al said happily as he continued kissing her inner thighs. "It's so nice to watch, but it makes me want to kiss you too."

"You're sweet!" Chong-kyu said. She reached out, ran her free hand into Al's hair and pulled him forward, pulling her other hand out of the way so he could kiss her. "Oh, Al, Oh, baby, that's so good!" she moaned happily, rubbing the back of his head with both hands.

"Mmm" Al hummed happily as he kissed.

"Oh, Al…" Ching-kyu moaned quietly. Then she let her head fall back on the pillow and just moaned softly as he kissed. Al ran his hands up her stomach to her breasts and began massaging them as he kissed her pussy. Chong-kyu arched her back. Al pressed harder with his tongue. Chong-kyu began rocking her hips and he picked up speed to match her rhythm.

"Oh, Al!" she cried out "Oh, baby, oh, Al, baby, you're going to make me come!"

Al's enthusiasm increased. He pressed his mouth on her pussy, licking vigorously and sucking gently.

Chong-kyu howled in ecstasy over and over. She brought her legs together clamping Al's head between her lovely thighs. "Oh, baby." She gasped. She grabbed him by the ears and pulled him upward. They had a long passionate French kiss. She reached down and grabbed his ass. But instead of guiding him into her, she pulled his hips upward. She scooted back so her head was propped on a pillow against the head board. She pulled his hips forward some more. Al looked slightly puzzled. Chong-kyu grinned up at him. "I want you to fuck my face!" she explained with a wink and opened her mouth.

"Chong-kyu, you are the first lady of good craziness!" Al told her with a wide smile.

Before she could answer 'I know', Al stuffed his erection into her mouth and began driving slowly in and out. Chong-kyu kept her hands on his hips until she had established the pace and depth she wanted. Then she reached one hand behind Al's ass to continue setting the proper pace. She slipped her other hand down between her legs so she could play with herself. Chong-kyu enjoyed the fun of pulling Al's hips forward and back so that his erection went in and out of her mouth, and the pleasure of playing with herself. The fun and the pleasure worked together to bring her right back to the edge of another orgasm. Al sensed it and began to pull back, but Chong-kyu held onto his butt and pushed him back into her mouth. "Ooooh!" she moaned through her full mouth as she came. Then she brought her hand up, grabbed the base of his erection, gave him another appreciative suck, and pushed him out. She looked up at him and said "Hey, baby, my pussy is jealous of my mouth."

Al just smiled. He scooted down between her legs, positioned himself, and plunged into her warm pussy. Chong-kyu threw her head back and gasped "Oh, baby!" she cried. Al began driving deep inside her, kissing the deepest part of her pussy with the end of his erection. He moved slowly, then fast, then slowly again. Chong-kyu let the feeling flow through her. "Oh, Al…oh, Al…baby…you're going to make me come again!" she cried. Al felt her pussy ballooning and drove hard and deep into her, sending her over the edge again and again.

When Al slowed to catch his breath, Chong-kyu recovered enough to say "Baby, my pussy needs a little rest…"

Al looked puzzled.

"Lie back a moment, you need a rest too. And I know just the way to rest."

Al slid out of her, and rolled onto his back. Chong-kyu turned around, got on her hands and knees, straddled his head, and sat on his face. Al began kissing her gently…she had said her pussy needed a rest after all. Chong-kyu leaned down and began sucking him slowly. Al moaned. She lifted her head, still stroking with her hand, bent down, and began licking his balls. "Oh, Chong-kyu, you are amazing" Al groaned.

"I know" she said playfully, licked a few more times, and began sucking again.

Al brought his head back up, and resumed kissing Chong-kyu's beautiful pussy with renewed enthusiasm. He grasped her ass cheeks, and began massaging. Chong-kyu moaned. Al knew he had found another thing she liked, so he went with it.

Chong-kyu moaned again. She lifted her head and said "Oh, baby, I think I'm going to come again!"

Al chuckled happily and kissed with even greater energy.

"Oooooh!" Chong-kyu moaned. She brought her mouth down on him again, trying to suck a little more before the now imminent orgasm hit her. She moaned through full mouth again, then pulled her head back, releasing his erection. "Baby, I'm going to come!" she shouted. She dropped her head down, howled with delight, and gushed onto his face.

Al coughed once, and then kissed Chong-kyu's pussy gently a few times before she rolled off of him. She lay on her back panting for a moment, then she held her arms up for a hug. Al rolled on top of her, hugged her, kissed her, and slipped into her pussy. They lay like that, hugging and kissing and making love slowly. Al began rocking his hips faster, and Chong-kyu moaned happily. She looked up at him and said "Want to try some back door, baby?"

"If you like…" Al said playfully.

Chong-kyu knew he really got a kick out of it, and she enjoyed it too. Besides what would around the world be without a bit of back door? She looked up at him as said "I like! Lube and condoms are on the night stand, baby."

Al slid out of her. He grabbed a condom, rolled it on, lubed it thoroughly, and scooted back to Chong-kyu, who raised and spread her legs. She rubbed her pussy with one hand and said "Give it to me, baby!"

Al pressed his well lubed erection against her back door. Chong-kyu smiled up at him. "In, baby…" she said softly. Al pressed part way into her back door. He rocked back and forth like that while Chong-kyu rubbed her pussy. "Kiss…" Chong-kyu said, again softly. Al bent down and kissed her. They had a long slow French kiss. Then Chong-kyu whispered "In, baby, all the way in…"

Al pressed gently. Chong-kyu felt relaxed and happy, so he slid right into her back door. Playing with herself helped. Concentrating on the wildness of it helped. And looking at the excitement on Al's face helped. Plus it was fun, and felt good in a special kind of way. The combination put Chong-kyu in a perfect groove, and soon she was on the verge of another round of orgasms. She gasped.

Al slowed for a moment. "Are you OK?" he asked.

"Don't stop, baby, I'm about to come!" Chong-kyu pleaded.

Al started thrusting faster. Chong-kyu rubbed her pussy faster. "Oh, that's good!" she cried. "Oh, baby, I'm going to come! I'm going to come!...Oh, baby! Oh, Al, I'm coming ahhhhhh!" she screamed.

"Oh, Chong-kyu, you're so amazing! You're so hot! Oh, Chong-kyu! Oh, honey! Now I'm going to come!"

"Give it to me, baby!" she urged. "I want you to come of my face!"

Al pulled out of her back door. He peeled of the condom and tossed it away as he scooted over to her face. He pumped his erections only twice before he shot a load across Chong-kyu's cheeks. She opened her mouth for him and he plunged his erection in as deep as he could. Chong-kyu sucked happily and hummed as he his next few shots went into her mouth.

When Al regained his composure, he pulled back, scooted down the bed, and slipped his still hard erection into Chong-kyu's beautiful pussy. "Oh, Al…" Chong-kyu moaned.

"Oh, Chong-kyu, you are amazing…"

"You like my pussy?"

"Oh yes!"

"Better than my back door?"

"Much better"

"Oh, your sweet…mmm, I think I might be able to come again…"

"Oh, Chong-kyu, my treasure, I love making you come." Al said and began rocking his hips again. He kissed her face and stroked her hair and held her tight as he made love to her. Soon he could feel her pussy ballooning again. He smiled to himself and kept the rhythm going. He felt her shudder and squeeze. He kissed her again.

"Oh, Al, baby…Oh, that was so sweet…" she said.

They lay together a long time, hugging, kissing, and just gazing into each other's eyes.

The Queen of Clubs

"OK, Al, I'm at your disposal, do with me as you will…" Chong-kyu said with a wink.

"Very good. Step one, take off your pants."

"OK" Chong-kyu said with a smile, slipping out of her jeans and panties in one swift motion.

"Now, hop up on the bed and get on your hands and knees."

"Oooo, am I going to get a spanking?" Chong-kyu asked with a naughty grin.

"Mmmm, something a bit nicer…"

"Nicer than a spanking? I can hardly wait!"

Al just chuckled. He stepped out of his own pants. He took the two vibrators from the box, and sat down on the bed so that he was facing Chong-kyu's shapely ass. He kissed each cheek quickly, and then turned on the vibrators. He ran the vibrators up and down Chong-kyu's thighs.

"Oooo, nice!" she said.

He ran the vibrators up the inside of her thighs, back down, and then ran them along the back of her thighs toward her perfect derriere. The gold vibrator he run back down her thighs, the silver one he ran back and forth across the top of her ass.

"Ooo, fun!" Chong-kyu said, knowing more was on the way. "Can I kiss you?" she asked.

"You certainly can!" Al answered happily. He ran the silver vibrator back and forth across Chong-kyu's magnificent ass, and pressed the gold one gently against the lovely patch of silky black hair in front of her pussy.

"Mmmm" Chong-kyu moaned as she took him in her mouth and began sucking.

Al continued running the silver vibrator across the top of Chong-kyu's lovely ass as he brought the gold vibrator back and moved it gently across the opening of her sweet pussy. Chong-kyu moaned and kept sucking. Al held the gold vibrator so that it lay along Chong-kyu's pussy and pressed gently. Then he slid the silver vibrator down so that it lay between the cheeks of her derriere. Chong-kyu moaned with excitement and began rocking her hips. So Al began sliding the vibrators back and forth. Chong-kyu gasped even though her mouth was full. He pressed the gold vibrator against her clit and silver one against her back door. She gasped again, this time more urgently, and began sucking harder. Al slid the gold vibrator up and down along her pussy and pressed the silver one against her back door. He positioned the gold one so that it was still on her clit but was ready to slide into her pussy.

"Ooooh! Oh, baby that's good!" she cried, taking him out of her mouth for a moment. She started sucking again and pushed backward so that the gold vibrator slid into her pussy and the silver one went part way into her back door. "Aaah!" she cried in ecstasy.

Al moved the gold vibrator in and out of Chong-kyu's pussy. He held the silver one with gentle pressure in the entrance to her back door. Chong-kyu was now alternating between sucking and groaning. When she relaxed her back door and the silver vibrator sipped in, she gave up on sucking, she just held his erection with her hand, lay her head on his thigh, and howled and howled with delight.

Chong-kyu managed to pump him a little more with her hand before simply letting the feeling carry her away. Al was sliding the two vibrators in and out in perfect rhythm. Chong-kyu began rocking her hips in time with the vibrators. She still held his erection because it excited her, but she couldn't do anything but rock her hips and ride the waves of ecstasy that flowed from her pussy and back door through her whole body. She moaned, groaned, and howled, and still he kept sliding the vibrators in and out of her.

Finally, she lost all control. Her body convulsed, she collapsed onto her side and rolled onto her back. Al let go of the vibrators and they popped out onto the bed. Chong-kyu lay shaking as after-shocks swept through her. "Oh my gosh! Oh my gosh!" she panted.

Al, began to move to kiss her, but she held up her hand.

The hand meant *give me a moment*. Al smiled. He loved to see her in that state, blissed out and relaxed.

After a few breaths, Chong-kyu held her arms out for a hug. Al scooted over and rolled on top of her. They had a long slow intense French kiss. Chong-kyu held him tightly. "Oh, baby…" she said.

"Fun?" Al asked mischievously.

"Oh, yes, very fun." Chong-kyu said. "I wish I could have made you come too, though. I like when we come together."

"We could try now." Al offered, pressing his erection against her thigh.

"Mmmm, let's see if we can." Chong-kyu said playfully, guiding him into her. They gave it a try. And, of course they were successful.

"Into the shower!" Chong-kyu commanded playfully.

"The shower?" Al asked.

"Don't ask questions, just do as I say!" she said with mock severity.

"As you command, my lady!" Al said with a bow. He stripped off his clothes and went to start the shower. As he washed, Chong-kyu entered the shower and stepped into his arms. They had a long hug and kiss.

Then she said "Enough of this nonsense, we need to WASH!" They washed each other in a very thorough and fun way. As Al washed her legs, he leaned forward and kissed the front of Chong-kyu's pussy. She giggled happily, widened her stance a bit and said "Kiss properly! You."

Al tilted his head so he could kiss Chong-kyu's lovely pussy the way she liked. She grabbed a handful of his hair, tilted his head back further, and ground against his face. "Yeah, baby! Make me come! I demand you make me come."

Al would have given his best villain chuckle, but his face was pressed between Chong-kyu's shapely thighs and all he could do was hum mischievously, which seemed to do the trick. Chong-kyu started gasping. Al kept at it with great enthusiasm. Chon-kyu grasped him by the ears and ground herself against his face. "Make me come!" she shouted grinding harder "I demand you make me come! I command you to make me come! I command it…I co-co-co Aaaaa! I'm COMING!" she shrieked. Her knees buckled, and Al caught her in his arms. He lowered her onto the shower floor, laughing.

"Hey! No laughing!" she commanded through her own laughs.

"Yes, ma'am."

"What?"

"Ah, no, ma'am!"

"On your feet!" she commanded, barely suppressing her delighted and delightful laugh.

Al stood up.

"Hands on the wall. Feet apart…farther…farther…OK, that's good."

"What now, my lady?"

"And now…The rusty trombone!"

Al laughed, and Chong-kyu made no effort to silence him. She knelt behind him, grabbed his hips and rotated them so his back was slightly arched. She reached between his legs with one hand and grasped his erection. With her other hand she pushed his ass cheeks apart. She began pumping his erection and licking his back door. "This is really weird." Al observed.

Chong-kyu swatted his ass. "Hush!" she said, and resumed.

Al decided to go with it. As weird as it was, it was fun, and it was really turning him on. He started groaning, and Chong-kyu started stroking faster and licking harder. "Oh, Chong-kyu, you are crazy fun!" he groaned huskily, "Oh, Chong-kyu…Aaaa!" he gasped as he shot his load.

"Fun?" she asked.

"Great fun. Shall we rinse and dry off?"

"Yes." Chong-kyu said decisively "But don't think we're all done. I get to come last this time!"

"As you wish, my lady." Al said with a bow.

They had the usual cuddly washing and drying and then went to the bed room. Chong-kyu piled the pillows in the middle of the bed. She took the gold vibrator from the box, kissed it and turned it on. She looked at Al and winked, "Now, lick my ass while I play with myself!" she commanded.

"Yes, my lady." Al said with a wide grin.

Chong-kyu lay down of the pile of pillows with her ass in the air. She started working her pussy with the vibrator. Al knelt behind her, found a comfortable position for his hands, and began licking Chong-kyu's ass, starting with her lovely ass cheeks, but moving quickly to her back door.

"Oh, yeah!" Chong-kyu enthused. "Oh, this is so hot!"

Al kneaded her cheeks with his hands and licked her back door as she played. Soon she was coming. He kept kissing and massaging until she let out a long groan and let go of the vibrator. He kissed each cheek once and went to the bathroom to wash out his mouth so he could kiss her.

When he returned he found she had picked up the vibrator again and was looking at it with a naughty smile. "I want to come again."

"You want me to make you come?"

"No, not yet, I want to make myself come, but I want you to watch."

"Wow, sounds hot."

She shot him a look.

"…my lady." He added.

"Very good. Now watch me make myself come."

Al watched as Chong-kyu put on a very naughty, very sexy, and very sweet show. He was so excited by it that he started getting hard again. He grabbed his cock and started stroking.

Chong-kyu noticed "Hey, what are you doing? I'm the one playing!"

Al chuckled and let go of his erection. It was hard to do, Chong-kyu was putting on such a hot show. Soon, without realizing it, he was stroking again. Chong-kyu was coming again so she did not notice at first.

"Hey!" Chong-kyu said when she was between orgasms and saw what he was doing.

Al stopped but said "It's hard to resist. You are so hot, and the show is so sexy."

"Oooh, you say the sweetest things. Come over here and let me kiss you while I play."

Al scooted over to her and offered his erection to her. She opened her mouth. He slipped in and she began sucking. She worked her pussy with the vibrator and sucked happily, varying speed and intensity until she was shuddering again. She opened her mouth to howl again as she came again and again.

Al stroked himself slowly as she gasped and let go of the vibrator. She looked over at him. "Are you about ready to come baby?" she asked.

"Pretty close" he admitted.

"Let's come together in a grand finale." Chong-kyu said, spreading her legs for him. Al scooted around, lay on top of her and entered her. They both gasped. They started rocking their hips together, moaning and groaning until they both cried out together in ecstasy.

They lay together a long time, feeling each other's hearts beating, kissing occasionally, and gazing into each other's eyes. Eventually they got up, took another quick shower together. They dried, climbed into bed, held each other and just enjoyed being together.

Stranded…Sort of…

"Al, baby, I have some bad news."

"What?"

"We've been robbed."

"What? That's terrible! We have to report it to the hotel…"

"Don't worry, I already reported it to the hotel, informed the police, and called the credit card companies. We should have new cards in a couple of days. But for now, we are kind of stuck."

"Damn, that's really a pain."

"Oh, don't get upset. We can turn it into an adventure. Let's have another cup of coffee and then take a walk and see if we can figure out how to raise a little cash."

"I could wire my brother for some money…"

"Nah, let's not take the easy way out. I'm sure we can find a more interesting way to get some cash."

"Hmmm, you seem to be up to something, Cheryl my treasure."

"Mmmm…Could be…"

XXX

As they walked along Broadway in San Francisco, Al eyed the various topless clubs that lined the street.

"Want to go in one of the strip joints, baby?" Cheryl asked.

"As long as you don't mind…"

"Why would I mind? Anyway, I made the offer, so you should know it's all right."

"Your logic is impeccable as always, my treasure."

Even though it was still mid-afternoon, there was a pretty good crowd. There were only three dancers in rotation, but the show was not bad. They both had a good time.

One of the dancers finished her set, left the stage, approached them, and offered them a private dance.

Cheryl looked her over and then said "Maybe in a bit. I want to see the other dancer first."

"OK, I'll come check with you again after her set. But hey, you're awfully pretty. We're having an amateur night tonight. You should consider entering the contest."

"I'll think about it." Cheryl replied. Then she turned to Al and asked "You don't mind, do you, baby?"

Al shook his head. "No worries, I know you have a bit of an exhibitionist streak. You can dance here tonight if you want."

"You're sweet." Cheryl said the Al, then she turned to the dancer and said "Why don't you sit with us and have a drink? You can tell me about the contest while we watch the last dancer."

"Sounds good to me!" the dancer said. She gestured to the waitress, who brought an $8 glass of grapefruit juice, which Al was happy to pay for.

Cheryl and the dancer discussed the rules of the contest while Al watched the dancer on stage. She was a large boned blond with enormous breasts who danced with enthusiasm, so Al did not catch much of Cheryl's conversation.

During her third song the dancer on stage, who had noticed how closely Al was looking at her, winked at him. Al turned to Cheryl and asked "Hey, honey, do you mind if I tip the dancer?"

"Of course not! Have fun!" she said. She dug in the pockets of her pants, pulled out a dollar, handed it to Al and said "Give her a tip from me too."

Al took the dollar, and putting it in his teeth, approached the stage. The blond dancer stepped forward smiling. She pulled Al's head forward and pressed his face between her breasts, capturing the dollar in the process. She let Al go, took the dollar and tucked it into her garter, and went to go get a tip from another patron. Later in the set she danced back to Al for another tip and the process was repeated.

"That looked fun." Cheryl said when Al returned to his seat.

"Hope you didn't mind…"

"Why would I mind? I want you to have fun."

"You want to try?"

"No, I'm good. Anyway, I'm getting tips on dancing from Alicia here." Cheryl said gesturing to the dancer sitting beside her.

Al nodded.

"Hey, Alicia, do I have to wait until tonight to try the dancing?"

"Well…no…in fact, if you want you can take my set, I'm supposed to go on next, but I don't mind waiting one out if you want to give it a try."

"Oh, wow! OK, I guess I will."

"Oh, but wait, Kara's set is ending, you'll need some time to get ready."

"Why? What do I need to get ready?"

"Well, a costume or something…"

"A costume for nude dancing? Non-sense!" Cheryl said with a laugh. Kara was leaving the stage, so Cheryl stood up, undid her pants, pulled off her pants, panties, sneakers and socks in one quick motion. She pulled off her shirt, undid her bra and threw them to Al. "Hold my stuff, sweetie!" she said with a smile, and bounded onto the stage. She began dancing, mixing elements of ballet with disco steps and some of the stripper moves she had seen Kara and Alicia use. The effect was stunning. Beyond that, she had moved outside the usual pattern the dancers set. They usually did their first number in bra and panties, their second number topless, and the final song fully nude. Aside from a small wrist watch and a scucii holding her hair, Cheryl was completely nude right from the start. The difference definitely caught the attention of the audience. People were on their feet almost at once waving dollar bills in the air. Cheryl pulled the scucii from her hair and slipped it onto her left leg as a garter to collect the money. She danced from one person to the next collecting the money. By the end of the first song she looked like she had a Christmas Wreathe around her thigh.

Al stood up with a dollar for her too. As the song ended she danced over to him, squatted in front of him, grabbed him by the sides of his head and gave him a big kiss.

"Hey! Don't touch the dancers!" the bouncer shouted.

She looked up from her kiss with Al and said to the bouncer "He's not touching me, I'm touching him. But if you don't like it I can stop dancing."

The audience glared at the bouncer, who backed down.

She kissed Al again.

"Oh, Chong-kyu, you are amazing!" Al said.

She gave him one more kiss, then Chong-kyu pulled the collection of money from her improvised garter and handed it to Al. "Hold the cash, baby." She said. She was back on her feet dancing before Al could even react.

He looked at the pile of bills in his hands. It was mostly singles, but there was a fair number of fives and even a few tens and twenties in the mix. He straightened the bills into stacks, folded them, and stuffed them into his pockets. He did not bother counting the money, he did not want to miss any of Chong-kyu's dance, which was, if anything, even more amazing than the first one. Again the money accumulated in Chong-kyu's garter. This time she had to drop some it off half way through the song because it was piling up so fast. Chong-kyu was covered with a thin film of sweat and was grinning wildly by the end of the second song, when she dropped another pile of money with Al.

"Having fun?" Al asked, somewhat redundantly.

"Oh, yeah!" Chong-kyu said breathlessly. "Are you enjoying the show?"

"Oh…yeah!"

"Love you, baby!" Chong-kyu said, kissed him, and went back to dance for the third song. She pulled off the scucii garter and tossed it to Al. She didn't bother going around the audience members, she just danced, and the folks in the audience threw money onto the stage.

Someone approached Al and offered him $100 for the scucii. "Fuck off" Al replied with a laugh.

Toward the end of the third song there was so much money on the stage that it wasn't safe to dance around. Chong-kyu leaned back against the brass pole in the middle of the stage. She swayed and rocked her hips in time with the music. She looked right at Al. He saw her mouth the words "Oh, my gosh!" and saw her body shudder slightly.

When the song ended Chong-kyu leapt from the stage and threw herself into his arms. "Oh, baby, that was so much fun!" she said breathlessly.

"Did you have an orgasm up there?" Al asked with a delighted laugh.

"Just a small one." Chong-kyu admitted with a smile.

"You are so amazing…"

Chong-kyu didn't answer, she just gave him a big squeeze. Then she got dressed. They walked to a booth in the back of the bar to count the money and laugh about the incredibly hot show Chong-kyu had just put on.

The dancers gathered up Chong-kyu's money. Alicia brought it to the booth while Ramona, the third dancer in rotation took the stage. After she had dropped the money on the table, Alicia sat with them to help them count it. "You know, Cheryl, you'll win tonight's contest easy! I swear, that was the hottest show I've ever seen on this stage, and I've been dancing here for five years. You'll win for sure!"

"I guess, but after that experience, I don't know, I don't think it would be as much fun a second time."

"Really? I still think you should do it for the money."

"I think I have enough. But maybe Al could dance a number?"

Alicia just laughed.

"You think he doesn't have the equipment? Check this out!" Cheryl said. She undid Al's pants before anyone could object, and whipped out Al's still semi erect johnson.

"Put that thing away!" Alicia whispered with alarm.

"What? Isn't it great?" Cheryl asked with a naughty smile.

"Very nice…" Alicia said nervously "but you can't wave your dick around in here."

"It's not mine, it's his."

"Cheryl, please! You'll get us all in trouble!" Alicia hissed.

Cheryl gave it one affectionate squeeze and then tucked Al's Johnson back into his pants.

Al had sat there with a stunned smile the whole time.

"You have to admit, it's a pretty great schlong." Cheryl said with a playful wink.

"Oh, yes, very nice!" Alicia said laughing but relived that Cheryl wasn't waving it around anymore.

"If you offer him $20 I bet he'd let you watch him jack-off." Cheryl said with a crazed grin.

"Ah…that's OK…"

"It's a great show! I've watched it a few times. $20 is a good price. It's worth every penny!"

"I'll trust you." Alicia said. She thought for a moment and then said "Hey, if you kids are into exhibitionism, you might try 'The Lucky Looking Glass' down the road."

"Why?" Cheryl asked.

"They have live sex shows, and they are always looking for new talent. Pay's not bad either…"

"Want to check it out, baby?" Cheryl asked.

"Sure" Al answered, intrigued by the idea.

Al and Cheryl made their way down the street to "The Lucky Looking Glass". The cover was normally $5, but was waived for couples. They made their way through the darkened audience area and found a seat with a good view of the stage. They ordered beers, and turned their attention to the sage. The couple performing was putting on a fairly good show. They were a bit older, looked a bit rough, like a biker and his girlfriend, but they were having fun together, and that helped. The spot light remained focused on the action so that people had a good view of his erection sliding in and out of her pussy even as the stage rotated.

"What do you think?" Al asked, sipping his beer.

"I think the girl is wearing too much make up. And the guy has too many tattoos. But it's still pretty hot. I bet he pulls out and jerks off onto her chest at the end."

"Why do you say that?"

"She has big boobs."

"Maybe, but I'll bet he comes on her face. They look pretty traditional."

Cheryl laughed "Traditional, huh?"

"Well, as traditional as you can be having sex in front of strangers…"

"Hey, baby, why are there those mirrors along the back side of the stage? They aren't really big enough to reflect much of the action."

"I think they're windows."

"Windows?"

"Sure, I think they're sort of like private booths for rent."

"Why would someone rent a private booth?" Cheryl asked, puzzled.

"Probably so they can jerk off while they watch the show."

"Ha! That's so crazy!" Cheryl laughed. "Hey, you want to try it out baby?"

"No, but if you want to go in one and play with yourself…"

"No, I'm good. I came already this afternoon. Remember?"

"How could I forget?"

"Oh, look, baby, I think they're about ready for the climax!' Cheryl said, pointing to the stage.

Sure enough, the guy withdrew and scooted around the side of his girlfriend, pumping his erection. He aimed at her breasts, groaned, and came onto her breasts. Then he turned and rubbed his erection on her face, squeezing a few more drops out. The lights went down, and the crowd cheered.

"Looks like we were both right." Al said.

"Traditional…I guess" Cheryl agreed with a laugh.

"So, what do you think?"

"I guess they don't allow anal sex here."

"Uh, I guess. I mean did you like the show?"

"I think we could put on a better show." She said with a sly grin.

"Shall we go see the owner?"

"Sure…it seems like fun."

They headed to the back of the room where a sign above a door read "Manager – Auditions". There was just a small desk in the corner and a mattress on the floor. The man behind the desks looked up at them. "Want to audition?" he asked with a grin.

"We want to perform, but we're not doing a free show just for you." Cheryl said simply.

"OK, OK, fair enough. But two things. First, I got to see what you got. So strip down."

Cheryl glanced at Al, who was clearly annoyed at the manager's tone of voice, "It's OK, baby, I got this." She said to him. The turning to the manager she said "Look buster, don't try to boss me around. My man and I are the hottest thing you've had here in a long time I bet. So if you want us to perform on your stage show some respect."

"No disrespect intended, I'm sure" said the chastened manager. "Now, would you please show me your body so I can be sure you're the type of kids we like to have around here?"

"Certainly" Cheryl answered. She slipped out of her clothes, handing them to Al. She turned a pirouette. Al handed her cloths back to her. She got dressed.

"OK, very nice. Now, what about your guy. Has he got a decent schlong? And can he get it up?"

Cheryl just smiled. She turned, undid Al's pants, pulled them down to his ankles, took his stiffening member in her mouth, and brought it to full mast in four quick sucks.

"OooooKay!" the manager said. "I have a time slot at 10 PM tonight. You get $300 for the performance, plus tips, if any."

Al cleared his throat. "We want 50% of the money from the jack-off rooms too."

"Hey…who do you think you are, John Holmes or something?"

"Do you want us on your stage or not?" Cheryl asked.

"OK, OK, 50% of the money from the jack-off booths. Plus tips, plus $300. Shit, you kids are the hottest stuff we've had around here for a while. That much is true. Tell you what, go have a drink on the house and watch the next couple. Crusher and Bubbles are good performers, but you want to see at least one more act so you know there's more than one way to do things."

The manger got them a couple of beers and brought them to a table near the stage just as the next act stepped onto the stage. Cheryl grabbed Al's arm. "Look at them!" she said "Isn't she beautiful?"

Al looked and did a double take. "Wow! She really is hot!" he said, then added "…Er, almost as beautiful as you."

Cheryl laughed. "Don't worry, baby! I know I'm beautiful."

The performers were each dressed only in tight fitting ARMY t-shirts. She was a slender lady of Chinese extraction with waist length hair and nice strong shapely legs. He was tall and thin with greying brown hair. She danced for a bit while he leaned on the brass pole. She danced really well, most people hardly noticed him smiling, watching, and slowly stroking his semi erect member.

After a song, she lay on the rotating stage, spread her legs slightly, and began playing with herself. A cheer went up through the crowd. He looked at her, still stroking slowly, and she looked at him, playing with her pussy more and more vigorously. She arched her back, still staring into his eyes, rubbing her pussy. She played like that through a song, and just as the next song came on she shuddered with an orgasm. He stepped forward, let go of his erection, buried his face between her strong shapely legs, and began kissing with obvious enthusiasm. She tossed her head back and groaned audibly above the music. She ran her hands though his hair and cried out again and again as orgasms passed through her.

Finally, she pulled him upward. She noticed that he was not that hard anymore, so she sat up and began sucking him with as much enthusiasm as he had shown while kissing her pussy. Soon he was hard again. She lay back and he plunged into her. She wrapped her arms and legs around him. He slid in and out of her slowly. Sometimes they French kissed, other times they were breathing too hard. They weren't just fucking on stage, they were clearly making love. They had been enjoying the exhibitionist thrill at first, but now seemed to have forgotten the audience. She was screaming with orgasms and holding him tightly as he thrust inside her.

When the music changed, they seemed to remember where they were. He slide out of her and she turned around to get on her hands and knees. He plunged his erection back into her pussy, grabbed her hips and began thrusting rapidly. She came a couple more times and then reached back and swatted his hip. He slipped out of her. She lay over a cushion with her ass up, and he began smearing lube all over his erection.

"I guess I was wrong." Cheryl said, wide eyed as the lady on stage spread the cheeks of her ass and her man slowly worked his erection into her back door. "Wow!"

He positioned himself so that the spot light could clearly show his hard erection sliding in and out of her back door. She began playing with herself, gasping "Fuck my ass, sweetie! Oh, yeah, fuck my ass!" She gushed with an orgasm. He slid back out just in time. He managed two strokes before he came all over her ass. He collapsed next to her. Cheryl could just see him kissing her face as the lights went down.

Cheryl looked over at Al. He turned to her. "What do you think?" he asked.

"I think we're going to have to do something pretty spectacular to top that."

"I think you're right."

XXX

They stopped at a leather boutique on the way back to the hotel to get some supplies. Al let Cheryl choose the costumes. She selected two leather masks that covered their entire heads leaving only their eyes and mouths exposed. She added mirror sunglasses. Next she selected a set of black boots that came up to her mid-thigh, a black leather mini vest, a set of black velvet gloves that reached above her elbows, and a black thong that had two quick release straps at the hips. She also bought an ash blonde wig. Al watched her make the purchases and just smiled. "What some leather jeans, baby?" she asked.

"No, I'll just wear my black denim jeans. No one will be looking that closely at me anyway."

"OK, that makes sense."

Cheryl paid for the costumes with some of the cash she had made dancing. "Is there a place I can do some tanning and get a wax job?" she asked the cashier.

The cashier directed her to a salon around the corner.

While Cheryl was getting her tan and wax job, Al stopped at a nearby pharmacy to buy condoms and lube. He had a pretty good idea of what Cheryl would want to do, and he wanted to be completely ready.

Back at the Hotel room they tried on the costumes. It was pretty easy for Al, he just put on the mask and adjusted the laces on the side to make sure if fit snuggly but not too tightly. Cheryl adjusted her mask with a little more room. She also cut a small hole, about 4 cm in diameter, in the back of it. Al looked on curiously at first, but with growing appreciation.

Cheryl got undressed. She put on the wig and then put the mask on over it, pulling a blond pony-tail through the hole in back. She put on the mirror shades, held her arms out to the side, and said "Ta-Da!"

The effect was amazing. With her slight studio tan, the full wax job, the mirrored shades obscuring her eyes, and the blond pony-tail, no one would guess she was Asian. She could be a petite Swedish babe with a deep tan for all anyone could tell.

Cheryl cut the gloves at the wrist and checked to be sure she could get them off her hands but leave the part that went up above her elbows. "Why did you do that?" Al asked.

"I like the long glove look, but I don't want to have to try masturbating with gloves on. It seems weird."

"Good point…" Al allowed.

They spent the rest of the afternoon practicing hiding condoms in Cheryl's boots and gloves. Al practiced rolling them on and off surreptitiously. Though he got several very hard erections and she got very excited and wet over the course of the rehearsals, they decided not to have sex. They wanted Al to have a huge, messy, explosive come shot on stage. Fortunately, Al had very good muscle control.

At about 7 PM, they had a light dinner. They were too excited to eat much. After dinner, as they sipped coffee in bed. Cheryl could hardly sit still.

"Are you OK, my treasure?" Al asked.

"Sure…just really excited, and a bit nervous. I want to put on a good show. I'm almost too excited."

"You'll do great. I'm the one who has to really perform. If I mess up…"

"I know, but you'll do great, you always do. I'm not really nervous, just over excited, I guess...Hey, baby, do you mind if I play with myself?"

"I could kiss you a bit if you like." Al offered.

"Oh, that's sweet! But I think I just want to play. Is it OK?"

"Sure!" Al said with a laugh. "You know I think it's pretty when you do that."

"Thanks, baby…mmmm….ooooh…mmm…" she said as she started rubbing her pussy.

"Oh, Chong-kyu, you are so awesome!" he said, smiling at her.

Chong-kyu tried to say something back but she just managed and excited moan. After she had brought herself to several orgasms, she allowed Al to kiss her and give her several more. It was just what she needed to relax and get in the mood for the evening's festivities.

XXX

Al and Chong-kyu walked arm in arm down Broadway. Al carried the small duffle bag with their costumes. Chong-kyu leaned on him. Every now and then she squeezed his waist and he squeezed back. "Are you ready baby?" she asked.

"Sure, more than ready. And you?"

"Yup…I was just thinking…"

"About what?"

"About that couple that performed this afternoon."

"Crusher and Bubbles?"

"No, the other one. They were really into it. They put on such a good show. I hope we don't have to go on after and act like that."

"Yeah, that would be tough…she was really something, huh?"

"I hope we're that good when we're that age."

"I have confidence in you, my treasure."

"You're sweet. I guess we should stay in practice." She said playfully.

"I like that idea, Chong-kyu, my treasure."

They had arrived at "The Lucky Looking Glass". Al opened the stage door for Chong-kyu and they entered.

XXX

They were dressed and ready to go as they waited for the act before them to finish and the announcer to call them onto the stage. Al looked OK in his black mask, mirror shades and black jeans. Chong-kyu was wearing her mask, mirror shades, the tight mini vest, the high gloves, the black thong, and her boots that came to the middle of her thigh. She looked stunning! They held hands and laughed nervously to each other.

At last the announcer called out "And now, exclusively on the stage of The Lucky Looking Glass, fresh from their tour of Scandinavia: Sven and Mistress Ingrid!"

The music stated. Chong-kyu quickly wrapped herself in a dark blue blanket from the hotel. She strode out onto the stage. A cheer went up from the crowd. She did a pirouette, allowing the blanket to swing out exposing her lovely ass. Another cheer from the crowd. She laid the blanket down on the cushioned rotating part of the stage so that she and Al would have clean place for their performance. Then she began dancing in earnest. The crowd roared with appreciation. Money stated landing on the stage. When the first song ended and the second began, Chong-kyu popped the releases on her thong and pulled it away. The crowd went wild at the sight of her freshly waxed pussy. She felt a rush of excitement and began dancing with greater energy. Money kept landing on the stage as she danced. She noticed several members of the audience get up and head for the private viewing booths. It was going perfectly. Even a few couples from the audience headed for the booths. She hoped there were enough booths for everyone who wanted one.

The song changed again, Cheryl changed her dancing technique to match the new music. Maybe next song she would move to the hard core part of the show, but for now she was just enjoying dancing and the admiring looks from the audience. As she danced she noticed that a few people were shouting something. She could not make it out at first, but as it got louder she could tell they were chanting "Show your tits! Show your tits!" She considered how to respond. Should she take off the mini vest, or should she make them wait? She was not sure, but then she got a great idea.

There was a micro phone lying on the stage. Performers could turn it on so the audience could hear them moan, or they could turn it off if they wanted to plan their next move. Chong-kyu bent over and picked it up. She turned it on. "What?" she said into the micro phone.

"Show your tits! Show your tits!" the audience chanted.

Chong-kyu made a slashing movement to the DJ with her arm and the music stopped.

"What?!?" she shouted into the mic.

"Show your tits! Show your tits!"

"SILENCE!"

The audience fell silent.

Chong-kyu placed her fists on her nude hips and began pacing back and forth on the stage. She had tremendous presence for a lady who wasn't wearing any pants. The audience stared. She raised the microphone to her face again. "How DARE you speak to me that way!" she barked.

The audience stared dumbfounded.

"You want to see my tits?"

"YAY!" the audience cheered.

"SILENCE!"

The audience fell silent again.

"If you want to see my tits you better show some respect, and ask properly!"

Chong-kyu paced back and forth a couple of times.

"If you want to see my tits you have to say 'Please, Mistress, show us your beautiful breasts', got it?"

The crowd mumbled the words.

"What?!?"

"Please, Mistress, show us your beautiful breasts!" they said in unison.

"That was WEAK!"

"Please, Mistress, show us your beautiful breasts!" they said louder.

"Say it like you mean it. Say it like you want to run to the private booths and flog your log!"

"PLEASE, MISTRESS, SHOW US YOUR BEAUTIFUL BREASTS!" the crowd chanted.

Chong-kyu grabbed the front of her vest and pulled it open, revealing her magnificent breasts. The crowd went wild. They were amazed, Chong-kyu's breasts were even more fabulous than they expected.

The music came on again and Chong-kyu stated dancing again. More people headed to the private booths. Chong-kyu felt a thrill run through her. It was almost time.

At the next music change she recognized the song she had specifically request for this moment. She lay back on the blanket and the stage began rotating. Chong-kyu ran her hands up and down her stomach and thighs a few times to warm-up, then she pulled off the gloves on her hands so she could play with herself. She felt the spotlight on her as she rubbed her pussy. The thrill was amazing. The crowd was cheering and hollering and throwing money. She rubbed her breasts with one hand as she rubbed her pussy with the other. "Ooooh" she gasped and arched her back. The thrill of the audience watching her was so intense that it almost interfered with the pleasure of masturbating. It almost made it harder for her to make herself come. Almost, but not quite. She shuddered with a quick orgasm. She was still aware of the crowd, but she was more aware of the pleasure flowing through her body. She slipped two fingers into her pussy and started working her g-spot. "Aaah!" she gasped, arching her back again. She worked her clit with one hand and her g-spot with the other. She writhed back and forth gasping "Oooh…oh, oh, oh….Ah!...Ah!...AAAAA!!" she gasped "AAAAAAAA!" she screamed as she had a great shuddering gushing orgasm.

This was Al's cue. He moved quickly to her before she cooled down. He buried his face between her legs, kissing her pussy with great enthusiasm, keeping Chong-kyu riding a wave of orgasms. She threw her had back and howled with ecstasy. He reached up and put his hands on her sweet breasts. Chong-kyu gasped again. She reached down, grasped the sides of his head and began grinding her pussy against his face. "Oh….oh…oh, YES!" she cried. She pulled upward on his head and he raised up onto his knees. Chong-kyu sat up, unfasted his pants and pushed them down and out of the way. She grabbed his stiffening member and began sucking frantically. She really liked sucking him; she nearly had another orgasm just from the sensation and fun.

Al stood up so he could get his pants off completely. Chong-kyu kissed him some more, playing with herself as she did. Al laydown beside her and they performed a very sexy side by side 69. After a minute or so, Al rose again to his knees. He wrapped his arms around Chong-kyu's waist, lifting her hips so that her legs lay over his shoulders. He stood up so still holding her by the waist. He kissed her pussy as she hung upside down kissing his erection. The crowd cheered, but they hardly noticed.

Al lay back down on the stage. Chong-kyu lay on top of him. They continued the 69 for a while. Chong-kyu raised her head. She leaned down, stoking his erection with her hand as she licked his balls. Al had to restrain himself from calling her name. The audience had to believe she was Swedish…or something like that. Chong-kyu, sensing Al could get over heated, went back to sucking him slowly. Then she had to stop because Al's kisses were starting to overwhelm her. She held his erection in her hand, slumped forward and groaned as another orgasm swept through her. She rolled off of Al onto her back. Al rotated around, positioning himself above her. She grasped his erection and guided him into her. She shuddered with pleasure. She was expecting it to feel good, but after all the other orgasms from her hands and his mouth, it felt incredible to finally have him inside her. She pressed her mouth against his neck. "Nnnnnnnnnn!" she screamed. He began rocking his hips slowly. "Nnnnnnnnnn!!" she screamed again. He picked up the pace. She threw her head back again. "Oooh, baby! Oh baby, YES!" she cried. Al kept thrusting, and Chong-kyu was carried away on wave after wave of orgasms.

When Al slowed a little to catch his breath, she recovered a bit. She whispered hotly in his ear. "Take me from behind, baby!" Al slide out of her. She rolled over onto her hands and knees. Al slipped back into her pussy. He grasped her hips and began thrusting again. Chong-kyu was carried away once more. Al had hit a rhythm where he could go on and on like that. And he did until Chong-kyu was lying face down panting. He placed his thumb against her back door, it sent a shock of pleasure through her that revived her energy. She began rocking her hips as Al slid in and out of her pussy and began rubbing her back door with his thumb.

"In, baby, in…"

Al pressed his thumb gently part way into her back door.

"In…baby…please IN!" she cried.

Al pressed his thumb all the way into her back door and Chong-kyu cried out in ecstasy. She rocked her hips as he thrust in her pussy and rotated his thumb in her back door. Chong-kyu had another orgasm and fell forward. She rolled onto her back and Al entered her again. As he drove deep inside her, she whispered in his ear "Back door, baby!"

Al rose up on his knees again. He pulled a bright green condom from the inside of her left boot, opened it and rolled it on. It was OK that people saw. They wanted the audience to see what was next, and they wanted them to see clearly. Chong-kyu raised her legs high above her head and spread them wide. "Fuck my ass!" she commanded.

Al said nothing. He just bent over, pressed his erection against her back door and rubbed it up and down a bit. Chong-kyu sighed with pleasure. Then she said "Come on, baby, fuck my ass!" Al stifled an appreciative laugh, one did not laugh at Mistress Ingrid. He worked his erection into her back door.

Ordinarily, Chong-kyu played with herself during back door sex so that she could have an orgasm. But for now she just enjoyed the thrill, and gave herself a rest. There were more orgasms coming, and she did not want to get exhausted. She glanced around. The audience was going crazy. What a wild time! She groaned again and shouted "Yeah, baby, FUCK MY ASS!"

A huge cheer went up from the audience.

The spot light was focused on her ass and everyone could clearly see Al's johnson sliding in and out of it. "Yeah, baby!" she said more quietly to Al "Fuck me in the ass! I love it!"

Al knew she loved the fun of it more than the pleasure, especially if she wasn't masturbating at the time. He also knew she was really enjoying the exhibitionist rush of doing it in front of a crowd. He leaned down and whispered in her ear "Chong-kyu, you are so awesome!"

"I know," she whispered back "now get ready for the next phase. I'm going to fake an orgasm, that will be your cue."

"Fake one?"

"Trust me, baby, I'm not missing out. If I needed another real one right now I would be playing, you know that. Just get ready."

"Yes mistress…" he whispered back with a quiet laugh.

The audience did not hear any of the conversation. They were cheering too loud.

Al raised himself up on his arms and continued sliding in and out of Chong-kyu's back door.

"Come on, baby! Give it to me!" she shouted. "Fuck my ass! FUCK MY ASS!! Oh, oh yes! Coming! YES!"

That was his cue. He slid out of her back door, rolled the condom off and discarded it. Everyone figured he would shoot his load. But Al and Chong-kyu had more planned. He crawled forward and lay his erection between Chong-kyu's breasts. She usually did not go for this move, claiming that only women with huge boobs should do it. But for the show it seemed right. She pressed her breasts together so Al could fuck them. Every now and then, when his erection came up she would lean forward and lick the end of it. After a while she let go of her breasts. He scooted forward. She opened her mouth for him. He plunged his erection into her mouth, fucking her face, a move she found to be great fun. She hummed happily, sucking and enjoying the cheers from the crowd

She took him out of her mouth and pumped with her hand. She looked up at him and whispered "Want me to stick my finger up your ass, baby?"

Al took a deep breath before answering "Not now, I'll lose it for sure. Maybe at the very end if you really want to and it seems right."

"OK, baby. Ready for the grand finale?"

"Sure, how about you?"

"Yes!" she whispered with a naughty grin.

Al scooted back down and she guided him back into her pussy. She was ready for it to feel great, and now that she was rested the pleasure hit her with renewed intensity. "Oh, baby, that's so good!" she cried. Al began driving deep into her pussy, filling her with pleasure. She felt her pussy ballooning again. She sensed that Al felt it too. He picked up the pace and Chong-kyu groaned and howled as she came over and over. Al kept at it until she thought she would go mad. "Oh, baby! Oh, baby, I'm coming!" she screamed as she shuddered and convulsed.

Al slowed to catch his breath, and Chong-kyu caught her breath. She rolled slightly to the side. Al raised up on his knees. He lifted her left leg up and rested it on his shoulder. He tucked a cushion under her hips for alignment and support, and drove back into her pussy. The crowd cheered. They had a clear view of Chong-kyu's fabulous body and Al's hard erection sliding in and out of her pussy. The pleasure and the thrill gripped her again. She began quaking and screaming as the orgasms ran through her. Al drove and drove inside her as she screamed and howled in ecstasy.

Even through the waves of pleasure, Chong-kyu could sense that Al could not last much longer. It was time. She reached down, slid Al's erection out of her pussy and guided it toward her back door. Al had a condom ready. He rolled it on just before plunging into her back door.

Chong-kyu could feel the heat of the spot light on her pussy. She reached down and began playing with herself frantically as Al drove in her back door. The sensations were amazing; the spot light, the audience, Al's erection in her ass, and her hand working her pussy. She felt a tremendous orgasm coming on. "Oh, baby, fuck my ass!" she cried "Make me come! Oh, baby! OH, baby, I'm going to come! Oh, yes, oh, baby, I'm going to come! I'm going to GUSH! I'm…COMING! YES!!" Chong-kyu's body convulsed violently with a huge orgasm as she gushed all over Al's leg.

Al slide out of her back door, rolling the condom off just in time. He barely got up to her face before he came explosively all over her mirror shades and black mask. Chong-kyu opened her mouth and caught some on her tongue. Al was shaking all over. Chong-kyu took his erection in her mouth and sucked appreciatively. She worked her pussy with her left hand and her back door with her right, having a few minor orgasms in the process. She grabbed his erection with her right hand, pulled it from her mouth, and began pumping it. She aimed his still hard member at her breasts. "Come again, baby!" she said. She jammed two fingers of her left hand up his ass, pressing on his prostate. Al groaned and shot another load onto her tits. He groaned and slumped forward as the last few shots decorated her chest. The house lights went down and the crowd gave them a standing ovation.

In the dark Al climbed on top of her and slid his still mostly hard erection into her pussy. "What are you doing, baby?" Chong-kyu asked quietly.

"I want you to get the last orgasm." He said

It didn't take long. The sweetness and intimacy of it in the darkness was enough to send her over the edge in one last sweet, gentle orgasm. Al gathered her in his arms and carried her off the stage.

XXX

The haul from the show was substantial. The owner of the club tried to short change them, and they were in no condition to argue. But other performers came to their assistance. Crusher and Bubbles threatened to beat him up, but the bouncers intervened. But then the two people in the ARMY shirts walked in off the stage, still wearing no pants, and threatened to leave and never perform on his stage again if he ripped off Al and Cheryl. And so he relented.

Al and Cheryl slept until noon even though it was not that late when they got to bed. Al made coffee and Cheryl counted the money. "I guess we better bring this cash to the bank and deposit it."

"Don't we need to keep some to buy tickets?" Al asked, sensing that he knew the answer.

"Oh, no, I found our wallets. I had left them in my bag all the time."

"I should have known!" Al said with a laugh.

"Are you mad?"

"Of course not! I guess you wanted an adventure."

"Not a bad one, huh?"

"Not bad at all." Al said. He leaned over and kissed her.

They made love slowly, passionately, and privately most of the afternoon.

Into the Future

Al sat in the window seat of the railroad coach, gazing out and thinking about Cheryl Pak. How would she react to the news? She had often said he should have other girlfriends beside her. It had been a little disorienting at first. He had assumed she was trying to break up. But she assured him that was not the case. Then he had thought she had another boyfriend. But that was not the case either. At least it was not at the time. She said she might at some point, but had no real plans. The main thing was that they lived in different cities, and neither was in a position to move. So there was no way they could get married. And as much as they enjoyed each other's company, they both sensed that marriage would not work between them; they were at once too different and too similar. She just wanted him to be happy. So they agreed that they would just not discuss the possibility of other people, even though they knew it was out there. Al never asked Cheryl about other men. It was none of his business, and more than that, he just didn't want to know. Cheryl, for her part, occasionally asked him about other women, and sometimes even scolded him if he said he had not seen anyone else while they were apart. "You're a man!" she said "Men need sex. You don't want to ruin your health do you? Go get some girlfriends! I won't be jealous, really."

"You are a strange lady, Chong-kyu." He had said each time, using her Korean name to indicate his affection for her.

"I know." She said playfully.

So he had gone out looking for women when he was home in Boston and Cheryl was home in Chicago. And he had found Zoe; tall, blond, artistic Zoe. He had mentioned her once to Cheryl. "Good job!" she had said, "That's all I need to know. Now I know you will keep your health so you can still visit me when we're old and grey."

"You are a very unusual lady, Chong-kyu." He had said with a laugh.

"I know. Now carry me upstairs so we can make love." She had said, jumping into his arms.

Al never mentioned Zoe again. Cheryl still asked him in general terms about his sex life in Boston, and he admitted that he had one, but he sensed that she didn't want details, so he didn't supply them. And he never asked her about her nights in Chicago. It worked out fine.

But now Zoe wanted to get married. And Al thought it might be a good idea. He could use the stability. But he didn't want to give up Chong-kyu. He loved her. And he sensed that she loved him, though they hardly discussed it. It was hard to imagine life without her.

Zoe was not the problem. Zoe had things figured out her own way. She was a concert violinist. She played for a very good orchestra in the Boston area. But sometimes she went on the tours to other cities. And Al knew there was a tradition of the conductor having his way with visiting musicians. Al had brought up the question of the tradition. "They don't still do that, do they?" he had asked.

Zoe laughed and swept her long blond hair back from her face. "Sure they do." She said "But it's no big deal. It's just kind of a tradition. A lot of conductors are gay anyway, so they are just going through the motions with visiting female musicians."

"Really? It seems kind of twisted." Al had said.

"Oh, honey pie, don't worry about it. I always make them use a condom. And it's just a tradition. But if I refuse, I might get a bad reputation and stop getting invited to perform in other cities. Is this a deal breaker for you?"

"Well…"

"Look, Al, you're the one I love. But I can't break this tradition. And it's only a couple of times a year anyway. Please don't make me choose between you and my concert career."

"OK…I get it…"

"You're so sweet. And anyway, I know you have a little sauce on the side.
And I'm OK with it. So I guess it works out even, right?"

"What?"

"CK Pak…"

"But, how did you…?"

"Your phone, silly. You left it face up last Thanksgiving. You got a text from
someone named CK Pak. I can't remember the content, I didn't look that
closely. But it said something about being wet and thinking of you."

"YOW! Sorry about that…"

"Oh, please…if I was upset I would have said something at the time. And then
I proposed to you on Christmas, remember?"

"I thought we had just agreed to get married, I didn't think you had proposed."

"Well, it was my idea. Don't tell me you're so old fashioned you think only
the man can propose!"

"No, no of course not. I just hadn't thought of it that way."

"Well, neither did I until just now. Anyway, the point is I think you're a
sweetie, and I think we're good for each other. So just don't short change me,
or embarrass me, and you can keep your little Korean cookie if you want."

"She's not…" Al began to object, but then caught himself. He was about say
that Cheryl was a lot more than just a cookie, but that would have been
exactly the wrong thing to say. That would upset Zoe.

"Not what?" Zoe asked.

"She's not Korean, she's American." Al said.

Zoe laughed. "Oh, Al, you and your fixation with citizenship. You're such a
nut." She said affectionately.

So, Zoe was not the problem. But how would Chong-kyu react to being the 'other woman'? Would her oft stated and demonstrated tolerance fail? Worst of all, would she be sad? He could understand and cope if she got mad. But the thought of making her sad was too much to bear.

The train pulled into Union Station. Al exited the train and walked down the platform. He was grateful that only ticketed passengers were allowed on the platforms these days. It gave him a few more minutes to compose his thoughts.

Cheryl was standing at the top of the stairs in the waiting room. She was wearing her usual jeans and a wind breaker. Her hands were in the pockets, but she pulled her right hand out briefly to wave to him. They had a quick hug, and then Cheryl disengaged and stepped back. She put her hands back into the pockets of the windbreaker. "How was the train, my dear?" she asked.

"Ah, fine. How have you been?"

"I'm good…"

Al moved to put his arm around her shoulders, but Cheryl stepped back. "I can do that here."

"What?"

"I can't walk like that or hold hands in the station."

"Why?"

"Let's get a drink, and I can explain. Also, you can tell me whatever it is that you said we needed to talk about when you texted me. OK?"

"Sure…"

Cheryl led them to a small bar room in the corner of the station. They ordered beers at the bar. Al carried them to a booth in the corner. When they were seated, Cheryl looked at him and said "So, what's up?"

"Maybe you should tell me. Something has changed for you…"

"I'll tell you in a minute. You mentioned some big news that we had to discuss in person. So tell me, please." She said seriously.

"OK…well, you know how you said I should look for other women?"

"Of course! I hope you found some. Celibacy is not healthy, especially for men."

"Well, I did."

"Zoe, right? Anyone else?"

"No, just Zoe in Boston, and you in Chicago."

"OK, so what's the big deal?"

"Well, Zoe wants to get married."

"Congratulations!" Cheryl said. She reached out and patted Al's hand. It was then that he saw why she had kept her hands in her pockets, and why she couldn't show affection in public. She was wearing a sparkling diamond engagement ring.

Al looked at the ring, looked up at Cheryl, and said with a half sad smile "Congratulations to you too."

"Thanks! So, I guess I don't have to tell you my big news now." Cheryl said with a smile, cocking her head slightly. "I hope you're not upset."

"As Bogie said, we'll always have Paris."

"Paris?" Cheryl asked expectantly.

"The line from 'Casablanca'…"

"Casablanca?"

"It's a movie. A man is saying good bye to a woman he loves. They had had a love affair in Paris."

"Oh, I see…I think…"

"Yeah, so we'll always have Chicago, and Dallas, and Seattle, and New York…"

"And New Orleans! And I think I'll be able to meet you in Atlanta this spring…"

"You mean…?"

"Yup, I got us tickets on the 'City of New Orleans' for tonight. It should get us there by morning."

"No, I mean…"

"What? You didn't think I was planning to give you up, did you?"

"Well…"

"Don't be silly!"

"What about your husband, or fiancé, or whatever?"

"No problem. He and his buddies take a twice a year trip to the Chicken Ranch in Nevada. You know, the famous brothel? I told him that was OK, as long as I get two weekends with you…plus whenever we can meet on business travel."

"And he's OK with it?"

"Sure, he gets to go to the Chicken Ranch, so why not? I heard those girls do some pretty crazy stuff."

"And you're OK with it?"

"Of course! That way I know there's no emotional connection."

"You are something else, Chong-kyu."

"I know. Hey, I think we better start heading to the platform. Our train leaves in about half an hour."

XXX

Cheryl had not even wanted him to carry her bags to the train. It made sense. Nothing in public to cause embarrassment for either Zoe or Brad, Cheryl's husband to be. Cheryl had gone to her roomette in the Pullman car near the front of the train. Al had taken a solitary coach seat. He looked out the window as the train pulled out of the station. He figured it would be one or two stops before Cheryl texted him to say it was OK to come and see her. In the meantime, he was content to wait and read and look out the window. The whole situation had worked out better than he had hoped…at least so far.

The text came almost as soon as the train had cleared Chicago city limits. Al got up from his seat and made his way forward to Cheryl's Pullman car. He found roomette number 8 and rapped gently on the door. Cheryl opened the door, spotted him, grabbed his wrist and pulled him inside before any nosey neighbors could spot him. Al gazed appreciatively at Cheryl. She had changed into a bulky sweater and pleated mini skirt that was vaguely reminiscent of a high school cheer leader uniform. "You like the look, sweetie?" she asked.

"I do. What's the occasion?"

"Just trying it out. I thought I might wear it during Mardi Gras."

"Makes sense…"

"Have a seat!" she said, indicating the guest seat in the corner. Cheryl sat one the main seat in the room with her knees together and her hands in her lap. "So, things worked out fine!" she said.

"They certain did."

"I knew they would."

"How were you so sure?" Al asked.

"Oh, I have my ways of knowing things…" Cheryl said. She lifted her leg so that her foot rested on the seat and grabbed her knee. The skirt fell out of the way.

Al was delighted, but not all that surprised, to see that she wasn't wearing any panties. "Oh, Chong-kyu, you are awesome!" he said with a broad smile.

"You like my new wax job, baby?" she asked.

Al looked more closely. She had waxed her silky black hair into the shape of a pair of lightning bolts emanating from the top of her pussy. "Fabulous!" he said with a chuckle. "You like getting the wax jobs?"

"It's fun…and it excites me to think how you'll react. It was so much fun getting into this costume and everything that I really wanted to play with myself."

"So why didn't you? You know I think it's sweet when you do."

"I wanted to wait so you could watch…you said you think it's pretty…"

"Of course, Chong-kyu, my treasure…" Al assured her.

"Mmm…" Chong-kyu moaned as she started rubbing her beautiful pussy.

"Wow!" Al said softly.

"Pretty?"

"Very"

"Take your pants off, baby." Chong-kyu instructed playfully.

Al took his pants off. His stiffening member flopped out. He grabbed it and gave it a few strokes.

Chong-kyu smiled and said "Come her, baby and let me kiss it."

As Al stepped over to her, Chong-kyu took a tube of sex lube and squeezed some into her mouth. She put down the lube, grabbed the base of Al's erection and guided it into her mouth. She hummed happily as she rubbed her pussy and sucked Al's erection, coating it with slippery lube. After a moment, she pulled her head back and pushed Al gently out of her mouth. She winked at him and said "I want you inside me, baby."

Al just smiled. He moved back around, positioned himself between her legs. As he moved to enter her pussy, Chong-kyu reached down with her free hand and redirected him. "Not my pussy, baby. I'm still playing with my pussy. Back door…"

Al chuckled "Oh, Chong-kyu, you are so amazing!" he said softly but emphatically.

"I know." Chong-kyu replied as she guide his erection to her back door. "Slowly, baby." She added.

Al slipped into the opening of her back door, pressing gently, sliding partly back, and pressing gently again. He was in no rush, it was fun and felt awesome. He kept sliding slowly and gently back in and out of the opening of Chong-kyu's back door. Chong-kyu moaned and smiled with excitement. She rubbed her pussy slowly and looked into Al's eyes. "Now, baby…IN!" she said mischievously. Al pushed gently against slight resistance, and slipped all the way into Chong-kyu's back door. "Oh, yeah!" she gasped happily, rubbing her pussy with greater urgency. "Oh, Al, give it to me, baby!" she groaned. Al began rocking his hips, and Chong-kyu began moaning in rhythm with his slow thrusts. "Oh, oh, yes!" she gasped as she rubbed her beautiful pussy faster.

"Oh, Chong-kyu, you are so HOT!" Al said appreciatively.

"Oh, baby…give it to me, baby…give it to me!" She whispered urgently.

"Oh, Chong-kyu, you are so amazing…"

"You like it, baby?"

"Oh, yes…and you?"

"I like it too!" Chong-kyu said with a playful grin.

"Can you make yourself come?"

"I could…but I want you to make me come." She answered with a wink. She stopped playing with her pussy, lifted her sweater and started rubbing her breasts.

"Should I…?" Al began to ask.

"Just keep doing what you're doing baby. I think it's starting to really work for me."

"Yeah?"

"Oh, yeah….Oh, baby, give it to me!" She said huskily. "Yeah, baby, that's it, fuck my ass…Oh, baby! Oh, Al baby, Oh yeah! Give it to me! Oh…"

"Oh, Chong-kyu…"

"Oh, Al, oh yeah…oh, that's it! That's it! OH, baby I think I'm going to come! Oh, Al! Oh, Al, fuck my ass! Make me come! Oh, Al, baby! I'm going to come! I'm going to come!" Chong-kyu gasped. "I'm coming! I'm coming! Aaaah!" she shouted and gushed with a great orgasm. She immediately reached down and started playing with her pussy franticly "I want to keep coming! Yes!" she cried. "Yes! Yes!" Her body convulsed over and over. "Oh, baby! Oh, Al, face!" she cried "face, baby!"

Al drove deep once more, pulled out slowly, and scooted quickly around so that he was over her face. She worked her pussy with her right hand and pressed on her back door with her left hand. It only took a few strokes for Al to explode across her cheek bones. "Oh, Yes!" Chong-kyu shouted convulsing again with excitement. She opened her mouth wide and Al directed the last few shots into it. She pressed once more on her pussy and backdoor, shuddered briefly, and lay back panting.

Al walked over to the roomette sink and washed his hands and erection thoroughly. He took a pair of towels from the rack, wet one of them, and brought them both back to Chong-kyu. She smiled happily at him as she wiped her face and dried it. She handed the towels back to Al. Then she reached out, guided his still semi erect cock into her mouth and gave it a few appreciative sucks.

"Wow," Al said "That was amazing. What made you think of something like that?"

"I wanted to see if I could have an actual back door orgasm." She said with a relaxed and satisfied smile.

"Was it what you hoped for?"

"Oh, much better. It was really fun!" she said. "Did you like it?"

"Of course! I always have fun with you, my treasure." Al sat down next to her. He put his arms around her and kissed her. A little romantic cuddling after wild sex always seemed to make them both happy.

XXX

After a light dinner in the dining car they came back to the roomette and folded the bed down. It was only about 9PM, but they felt like climbing into bed together. The cuddled and played in a random way, just enjoying each other's company. They were in no rush.

After a while Cheryl asked "Hey baby, when do we pull into the next station?"

"Hold on…" Al said, He reached down to the floor, opened his gym bag, and pulled out the time table. He consulted it briefly and then said "We pull into the next station in about ten minutes actually."

"Hmm, do you feel like doing something crazy?"

"Sure, what did you have in mind?"

"Let's make love with the shades open."

"We could get in trouble…"

"Oh, don't be silly. We'll leave the lights off. No one will know for sure except us."

"OK, if you're up for it."

"Yay!" Cheryl climbed out of bed. She locked the door, slipped out of her t-shirt and panties, and raised the shade. It was dark out and they could see the country side rolling by. Al was lying on his back, so she straddled his face and lowered herself so he could kiss her. She leaned forward, pushed his shorts out of the way, grabbed his member, and started kissing it.

Al moaned and began rubbing Cheryl's back and ass as he kissed her. Cheryl moaned happily and chuckled to herself as her fiendishly fun plan fell into place. She felt the train beginning to slow. She got up on her hands and knees, turned to Al and said "Time take me from behind, baby!"

Al got up onto his knees. He rubbed her shapely ass cheeks, then he rubbed the end of his erection up and down on the opening of Cheryl's pussy. "Nice!" she said, then she slid backward so that she took his erection deep into her warm beautiful pussy. "Oooh, nice!" she said playfully.

Al slid in and out of her, gripping her hips gently. He just took things easily. He was having a grand time, but he sensed that Cheryl had a few more ideas she wanted to try.

The train slowed further as it pulled into the station. Cheryl shifted around on the bed, with Al still inside her. She put her hands on the upper edge of the window and scooted forward so that her face was hidden, but her lovely breasts were practically pressed against the window. Anyone looking closely would even be able to see Al's erection sliding in and out of her pussy. The train came to a stop in a place where the light from the station was at least not shining directly into the window. It was just right. People who looked would see them making love, but only if they looked closely. Cheryl stole an occasional glance out the window to be sure that at least a few people were enjoying the show. Eventually all the passengers who needed to had boarded or disembarked, the train started rolling slowly out of the station. Cheryl saw a group of college kids notice them and point. "Turn on the light, baby!" she said quickly.

"Turn on the light!"

Al reached behind him and flipped the light on as the train gathered speed. The college kids on the platform got a perfect view of Cheryl's breasts, pussy, and thighs. If they were paying attention, and they were, they could see Al's impressive erection plunging into her pussy over and over. The thrill of it sent Cheryl over the edge. "Oh, Al! Oh, baby!" she cried. He brought his hands up to her breasts. "Oh, YES!" she gasped and she came again. "Oh, baby!"

She collapsed onto her front. The train had pulled out of the station, so Al turned the light back off. He continued to drive deep into her soaking, sweet, hot pussy. "Oh, Al…" she panted. "Oh, baby, that was so fun…"

"It was…great fun." Al agreed and he slid in and out of her.

Cheryl turned her head and looked out the window. There was a college sports team bus running next to them. Light from the street lights was shining in the window. One of the kids on the bus noticed what they were doing and pointed it out to his friends.

"Al, turn the light on again!"

"Oh, Chong-kyu, you are amazing!" Al said appreciatively as he flipped the light back on. Chong-kyu felt another exhibitionist thrill run through her. She lay there with her ass up so Al could drive deep into her pussy. She could see the kids in the bus going wild. She knew the bus would fall behind as the train gathered speed. She let herself have one more quick orgasm, then she turned to Al and said "Quick, Al, come on my face again!"

"Already?"

"Yes! Before the bus pulls out of range! Let's give them a show they'll never forget!"

Al slipped out of her. Chong-kyu rolled over and opened her mouth. Al scooted up so he was straddling her chest. He pumped his erection furiously. "Give it to me, baby!" Chong-kyu urged him.

"Oh, Chong-kyu!" Al called as he shot his load all over her face and into her open mouth. "Oh, yeah!"

Chong-kyu grasped his erection and pulled it into her mouth so she could suck it as the bus began losing ground and faded into the night.

XXX

The train was stopped in a station somewhere in the south when Al slowly woke up. It was dark. There were a few people on the platform outside. A taxi driver helped a passenger with his bags.

Al's mouth was dry. He slowly eased his way out of bed. He looked at Chong-kyu and marveled at how lovely she looked sleeping. He bent over and gave her a gentle kiss. He pulled his shaving kit from his bag and headed down the aisle of the train to the rest room at the end of the car. While he was there, he took the time to shave and brush his teeth. He took one more drink of water and headed back to the room.

As he closed the door behind him, Chong-kyu sat up in bed. "What time is it, baby?" she asked.

"Not sure…I left my watch in my bag. I could check."

"No, that's OK. Hey, which way is the rest room?"

"Men's room is at the front of the car, Lady's room is at the back."

"I'll be right back." Chong-kyu said. She pulled on a robe and headed out the door.

Al climbed back into bed. He looked out the window at the country side rolling past. Telegraph wires rose as they approached the poles and then fell again between them. The effect always made Al smile. He was relaxing and looking at the darkened tree line in the distance when Chong-kyu slipped back into bed with him. She snuggled up against him. He kissed her on the fore head. "I love you." He said matter-of-factly.

"I love you too, baby." Chong-kyu said simply. She rested her head on his shoulder and gazed out the window for a while. "The train's nice, don't you think?" she asked.

Al turned and looked at her. She was so beautiful. "Yes" he said, and kissed her. He kissed her forehead, then her nose, then her mouth. When he kissed her mouth a second time Chong-kyu responded and Al was reminded of how exciting a French kiss could be. They held each other tight. Their legs intertwined. Al started getting hard, and his erection pressed against Chong-kyu's thigh. She began struggling out of her panties, and Al began struggling out of his underpants. Chong-kyu broke the kiss just long enough to moan "Oh, Al!" as she guided him into her.

Al groaned and drove slowly into her. "Oh, Chong-kyu…I love you!"

Chong-kyu shuddered and arched her back. "Al, baby, I love you too! I love you so much!" she gasped. She wrapped her legs around his waist and pulled him tight against her.

They rocked their hips in rhythm and ground against each other. They gasped and groaned and called each other's names. They French kissed when things slowed down, and breathed heavily in each other's ears when things sped back up. Al drove deep inside her tight, hot, soaking pussy. "Oh, Chong-kyu, my treasure, Oh, Chong-kyu, my love…" he breathed softly in her ear. He began kissing her neck.

"Oh, Al!" Chong-kyu gasped "Oh, Al, I love you…I love you so much!"

Al felt her pussy ballooning and felt himself getting much harder. He reached down to massage Chong-kyu's shapely ass, but she grabbed his hand and pulled it back up. Interlacing her fingers with his. "Let's come together, baby!" she said dreamily.

Al looked into her eyes, he wanted to say something but couldn't form the words. He brought his mouth down to hers and they began French kissing again. Chong-kyu began sucking his tongue. Al's whole body began to shake.

Chong-kyu broke the kiss so she could throw her head back and howl with a shattering orgasm. She could hear Al roaring as he came inside her with great convulsions. The sensation pushed her into even stronger orgasms.

Al thought he was never going to stop coming. Chong-kyu's pussy gripped him, her arms and legs held him tight, and their bodies shuddered together. At last the shaking stopped and Al slumped forward on top of her. He breathed hard as aftershocks flashed through their bodies. When he had regained some control, he lifted himself up on his elbows and began gently kissing her face.

"Aaaaah" Chong-kyu sighed.

"I love you, Chong-kyu." He said softly.

"I love you too, Al." she murmured quietly.

Eventually he rolled off of her. They lay side by side, kissing and cuddling as they regained their breath. The morning sun was streaming through the window by the time they finally got out of bed to get cleaned up for breakfast.

When the train pulled into New Orleans they caught a cab to their hotel and got dressed to explore the town. Mardi Gras celebrations were already starting up, even though it was still morning. So Cheryl put on her cheer leader outfit, including thong panties this time, and they headed out to join the festivities.

The streets were already full of people, many already drunk. There was singing, dancing, and lots of flashing. The protocol was fairly simple; men carried strings of beads, a woman would flash her breasts, and a man would give her a string of beads as a reward. "Would you be mad if I bought some beads?" Al asked.

Cheryl laughed "When in Rome…" she said.

Al went to a street vendor and bought a large bag that held about a hundred strings of beads. "It's the only size they had…" he explained.

"Then you should have bought two!" Cheryl said with a laugh. "Hey, give me a couple of them." She added.

Al handed her a couple of strings of beads. She ran over to a woman wearing a leather bikini top, cut-off jeans, and several strands of beads. She waved the beads at her. The woman shouted "Wooooo!" and pulled her bikini top out of the way, showing her ample breasts. Cheryl draped a sting of beads around her neck. The woman then held out a set of beads toward Cheryl and raised her eyebrows. Cheryl gave a quick look to Al, who nodded with a smile. She lifted her sweater.

"Woooooo!" the woman in the leather bikini shouted again. She draped some beads around Cheryl's neck and gave her a kiss on the cheek. "Hey, hon', is that your man?"

"Yup!"

"Come here, hon'" she said to Al.

Al walked over.

"First flash of Mardi Gras?" she asked Cheryl.

Cheryl nodded.

"Well, let's get a picture to commemorate it!" the woman said. She pulled her bikini top out of the way again, and put an arm around Cheryl's waist. Cheryl lifted her sweater again so that Al could get a picture. "Woooo!" the woman shouted again and wandered off into the crowd.

"What do you think, Al, baby?"

"I think you are awesome, Chong-kyu!"

"Wooo!" Chong-kyu shouted, and flashed her breasts at him. Al gave her another string of beads.

As the morning progressed Chong-kyu gathered an impressive collection of beads, even as she and Al handed out many many strings to other ladies who were flashing. Chong-kyu also discovered that she could get strings of beads by lifting up her skirt to show her shapely ass.

At mid-morning Chong-kyu turned to Al and said, "Hey, baby, it's getting too hot for this sweater."

"Do you want to go back to the hotel and change?"

"Actually, I was thinking of going to one of the body painting places. Do you mind?"

"When in Rome…" Al said with an appreciative laugh.

They found a lady doing the body painting right on the side walk. There were several other ladies waiting in line. Chong-kyu was hot, so she took of her sweater while she was still in line. No one seemed to mind.

When she got to the front of the line, the lady washed her chest, dried it, and studied it. "For you, we need something really elegant that doesn't hide the shape of your breasts."

"Why?" Chong-kyu asked.

 "Because you have beautiful breasts, silly!" the lady said.

After a moment of consideration she airbrushed Chong-kyu's chest royal blue. Then she took some gold paint and drew a stylized sun over her right breast and a stylized moon over her left.

Al whistled, paid the artist, and took a picture. They walked off into the crowd, gathering approving stares and giving away strings of beads to big breasted women who flashed them. By early afternoon they were nearly out of beads (Chong-kyu had started giving away the beads she had gotten, she didn't need them, and anyway it was fun), and they were getting hungry. They could not go in a restaurant with Chong-kyu wearing nothing but paint above the waist. Street vendor food was expensive and low quality, so they went back to their hotel room and ordered room service. The kitchen said it was about an hour wait, but they said that was OK. Al went down the hall to the vending machine, returning with two bottles of lemonade.

As they sipped the lemonade, Chong-kyu said "Hey, baby, want to hear something funny?"

"What?"

"I'm feeling insecure about my breasts."

"What? You…of all people…feeling insecure? I didn't think you knew the meaning of the word!"

"Hey, I'm secure enough to admit when I feel insecure."

"OK, what can I do to help?"

"I want you to worship my breasts."

"OK" Al said. He stuck his arms out and made the bend at the waist motion that pantomimes people worshiping an idol.

"Not like that, silly!"

"How?"

"Take off your pants, look at my boobs, and jack off, silly!"

"OK" Al said, taking off his pants "But it seems like a waste. Shouldn't I do something that will get you off too? I could kiss them and then kiss your pussy."

"Maybe after…for now, I want you to just admire my boobs and jack-off."

Al smiled and shrugged. He grabbed his slowly stiffening member. It got super hard after only a few strokes; Chong-kyu's breasts were so sexy. After a minute he stepped forward toward her.

"What's up, baby?" she asked.

"Your boobs are so amazing! Can I come on them?"

"Do you want to?"

Al nodded emphatically.

"How badly?" Chong-kyu said with a teasing laugh.

"I would hold my hands out wide to show you," Al said "But I don't think I can stop pumping my erection!"

"OK, then…let me have it! Jack off onto my boobs!"

Al stepped forward, aiming at Chong-kyu's breasts. A morning of excitement, mostly generated by Chong-kyu, followed by looking at her boobs and jacking off, worked together to create a huge messy load that he shot all over Chong-kyu's breasts. "Yahoo!" Al shouted.

"Woooo!" Chong-kyu shouted in response.

They went to take a shower together. Al washed the come and the body paint off of Chong-kyu's chest. They washed each other, and then Al washed and kissed Chong-kyu's breasts some more. They dried each other, and then he carried her to the bed. He lay her down, and began kissing her pussy. Chong-kyu ran her hands through his hair. He reached up and put his hands on her breasts. She sighed with pleasure. As his enthusiasm increased, Chong-kyu's pleasure increased. Soon she was moaning and groaning and gasping. "Oh, my gosh!" she panted. "Oh, baby, that's so good!" Al just got more excited and kissed better and better. Soon she was shaking with orgasms. Her thighs clamped around his head. She grabbed a handful of his hair, pulling him up to her face so she could kiss him. She felt that he was hard again, so she happily guided him into her. She threw her head back and groaned loudly as he slid deep inside her. "Oh, my gosh!" she gasped "Oh, baby, you're going to make me come again!" Al said nothing. He reached down, pressing his little finger and ring finger on her clit and his middle and index finger on her back door. Chong-kyu tumbled over the edge, screaming as a massive orgasm ran through her. Al kept driving deep inside her, and she kept coming. When he slowed a little to catch his breath, she looked up at him and said "Are you ready to come, baby?"

"I just came a while ago. I'm in no hurry."

"But the food will be here soon."

"Chong-kyu, my treasure, I don't need to come again right now. I can save it for later this night."

Just them there was a knock on the door. "Room service!"

"Just leave it, we'll get it in a minute." Chong-kyu called.

They had along slow French kiss, and then Al got up, wrapped himself in a towel, and got the food.

XXX

After a leisurely lunch and a long nap, they were ready for an evening of fun. Cheryl wore her thong and cheer leader skirt again, but this time she wore a light t-shirt; no bra of course, she planned to flash her breasts…a lot. Al bought another bag of a hundred strings of beads, and they headed out for fun.

As the night progressed Al's supply of beads decreased, and Cheryl's increased. At about 10PM, as they walked down a street where things were getting pretty wild, Cheryl spotted someone she knew. "Al, come on, I want to introduce you to someone." Cheryl said as she took his hand and pulled him forward.

"Darla!" Cheryl called.

A blond lady in a tube top turned and a delighted smile broke across her face. "Cheryl?!"

"What are you doing here?" Cheryl asked.

"Showing my tits to strangers!" Darla said with a laugh, pulling her tube top down to reveal her great big breasts. "Woooo!" she shouted. "How about you?"

"Same thing!" Cheryl laughed, lifting her shirt. "Hey, let me introduce my man! Darla, this is Al. Al, Darla. We were roommates at the University of Chicago."

"Nice to meet you." Al said, trying, with only partial success to look in her eyes.

"Nice to meet you too. Hey, this is Ralph, my guy. Ralph, this is Cheryl Pak, my old roommate, and her beau Al."

Al and Ralph nodded to each other and shook hands.

"Hey, where you guys headed?" Darla asked.

"Nowhere special…" Cheryl said.

"Well, come with us. There's supposed to be some wild stuff going on two blocks from here."

So they followed Darla and Ralph. Things were pretty crazy; many of the women had taken off their tops completely, some were totally nude. Even some of the men were naked, but fortunately not many. There were groups of women dancing topless in the middle of the street.

"What's going on over there?" Cheryl asked, pointing at a small crowd gathered around a street lamp.

Darla ran over to check it out. She came back laughing. "Some crazy lady's giving her boyfriend a blowjob…in public!" she announced. They all had a good laugh and continued down the street. Darla and Cheryl flashed their breasts at a few people, and collected some beads, but in the general madness of the street it didn't cause much of a sensation. It was fun, but they all sensed that there was something more in the offing. As they turned a corner, Darla spotted a perfect opportunity. There was an old police car parked in front of a bar. She grabbed Cheryl by the wrist, shouting "Come on!" Cheryl followed, puzzled but willing. The men followed too, knowing something cool was afoot. Darla climbed up onto the trunk of the police car and began dancing. "Come on up!" she shouted to Cheryl.

Cheryl looked over at Al and raised an eyebrow.

"When in Rome…" Al said with a laugh.

Cheryl jumped up onto the hood of the police car.

Darla, who had great big breasts but an unremarkable body otherwise, pulled down her tube top so she could dance topless.

Cheryl, who had a stunning body all around, stripped down completely, tossed her clothes to Al, and danced nude.

They danced to the music blaring from the door of the bar. A bunch of folks from the bar came out to the side walk to enjoy the show. Cheryl danced with great style and energy. The crowd grew in both size and enthusiasm. After a few songs, Darla, who was not in as good shape as Cheryl, sat on the trunk of the police car and beckoned Ralph to joiner her. She unfastened Ralph's pants and lay back against the rear window of the police car. Ralph lay his erection between her breasts, pushed them together, and started titty fucking her. The crowd roared with approval.

Not to be out done, Cheryl caught Al's eye and gestured for him to climb up on the hood of the police car. Al climbed up. Cheryl undid his pants, shoving them down to his ankles and helping him step out of them. She grabbed his rapidly rising erection and began sucking it with abandon. The crowd roared with approval. She looked up at him and winked.

"Oh, Chong-kyu, you are so amazing!" he said.

Chong-kyu took his erection out of her mouth. "I know!" she said as she pumped it with her hand. She went back to sucking with even greater enthusiasm.

Al knew that this performance, fun as it was, was a lot of work for Chong-kyu, so he should come soon. He let awesome blow job and the excitement build up quickly. As the pressure began nearing the breaking point, he said "Hey, honey, should I come in your mouth?"

"Uhn-Uh!" Chong-kyu said shaking her head slightly as she sucked.

"Face?"

"Uh-huh!" she said with a slight nod.

"You're so awesome!" Al said.

"Uh-huh!" she said again nodding slightly.

"Want to play with yourself while you do that?" Al asked hopefully.

"Uh-huh!" she said nodding slightly a third time. She reached down between her legs and started rubbing her pussy.

That was all it took, Al was ready. "OK, honey, I'm about to come…I'm about to…I'm about to… I'm going to come!"

Chong-kyu pulled back in time to catch most of the load on her cheek bones, some in her open mouth, and some on her beautiful breasts. She immediately stuffed Al's erection back into her mouth and sucked vigorously, catching the last few shots in the back of her mouth. She hummed happily and sucked some more for a few seconds. Then she pulled back, kissed the end of his erection, and stood up. Al handed her skirt, thong and t-shirt to her. She hopped down from the hood of the police car and got dressed while Al pulled his pants up. Darla arrived a moment later with some Kleenex from her purse so Chong-kyu could wipe her face. Al hopped down next to her and gave her a big hug.

"You're amazing, Chong-kyu, just amazing." He said.

"I know! Hey, let's go get a drink. That was fun, but I don't like the after taste so much."

"As you wish, my treasure." Al said.

They walked a couple of blocks, looking for a place to get a drink. Chong-kyu was having fun, but she was ready to be a bit more of a spectator for a while. Darla, on the other hand, did not bother to pull her tube top back up. She seemed to be enjoying the admiring glances she got from the passing crowd. There were only a few after hours places still open.

Darla spotted one that had a big sign above the door proclaiming "LIVE SEX SHOW!!"

"Let's try that one!" she recommended.

"OK," Chong-kyu said. She turned to Al and whispered "Let's just watch this time."

"As you wish, my treasure. I don't think anything could come close to our performance is Frisco."

"I know! Right?" Chong-kyu said "Besides, we don't have our costumes."

"Quite so…" Al said. He didn't mention that they had not had their costumes on top of the police car either. He figured Chong-kyu knew that already. Anyway, he was in the mood to just watch for a while too.

They found a booth with a good view of the stage and ordered whisky on the rocks. When the drinks arrived, Chong-kyu pulled the ice cubes from Al's drink and added them to her own. She liked a lot of ice in her whiskey, Al preferred his straight. They tossed back the first round of drinks and then nursed a second round as they watched the couples on stage perform. For the most part they were either enthusiastic but lacked imagination, or showed imagination but lacked enthusiasm. Chong-kyu guessed that many of the female orgasms were faked, and she could swear that one woman was even chewing gum as her man fucked her in the ass; entertaining, but not very exciting. Still, they were all having fun. Darla and Ralph had never seen a live sex show before, so they were fascinated.

Lesbian couple came on later in the evening. Their show was pretty, but it didn't do much for Chong-kyu, she never saw the appeal of girl-girl porn. When another biker and girlfriend couple climbed onto the stage, Chong-kyu slipped her hand into Al's pants and pulled his hand up under her skirt.

"Is the show turning you on, my treasure?" Al asked as he rubbed her pussy.

"Not especially," she answered, stroking his Johnson, "I just thought it would be fun to play a bit."

"I can't disagree…" he replied.

They played with each other through the biker and girlfriend performance. It made things more interesting.

Darla yawned, and Chong-kyu was about to suggest they leave, when the next act stepped into the spot light. It consisted of a beautiful young lady, who seemed to be a mix of French and Chinese ancestry, and two guys, one muscular with black hair, and the other tall with blond hair and big hands, that promised something else big. "Let's stay for one more." Chong-kyu suggested. Darla readily agreed. The guys were OK with it too.

The two men kissed the young lady all over her body, starting with legs and back and working their way around until they were kissing her breasts. She seemed to be enraptured, swaying with the music and moaning audibly. The men laid her on her back. The black haired man kissed his way down her stomach to her pussy. She leaned her head back, letting out a long groan of pleasure as his mouth arrived at its destination. The other man, the blond, stepped out of his shorts. His semi erect johnson flopped free. Sure enough, it was very impressive. He offered it to the girl, who took it in her mouth and sucked with obvious relish. After a minute or so, the black haired man stood up and slipped his rock hard erection into her pussy. The young lady moaned and began sucking the blond man harder as the black haired man drove in and out of her pussy.

Chong-kyu began grinding against Al's hand. He helped by rubbing with his fingers. He leaned over and kissed Chong-kyu on the side of her head. She squeezed his johnson in response.

The black haired man slipped out of the young lady's pussy, climbed up, lay his erection on her chest and, when she pushed her breasts together, started fucking her cleavage. The blond haired man pulled his now fully hard erection from her mouth. He walked around her and slipped into her pussy. She gasped, groaned, and moaned over and over. He groans gathered intensity as the blond man drove his large erection in and out of her pussy. She let out a great cry as she came. She grabbed the black haired man by his ass cheeks, pulled him forward, and began suck him vigorously. The blond man kept driving deep in her pussy, and soon she had to stop sucking so she could scream again.

Chong-kyu was grinding harder against Al's hand. He just smiled and went with it.

The blond man slipped out of the young lady's pussy and helped her roll over. He switched positions with the black haired man, who now entered her pussy. She moaned over and over as she sucked the blond man's erection. She stopped sucking soon enough, holding his erection in her hand as she howled through another series of orgasms. The black haired man withdrew from her pussy and she crawled up on top of the blond man. She guided his massive erection into her pussy while the black haired man rolled on a bright green condom. Sure enough, he knelt behind her, leaned forward, and pressed his erection into her back door. "Oh, YES!" the young lady cheered as he entered.

Chong-kyu was grinding vigorously against Al's hand, soaking right through her thong. Al kissed her neck. He considered whether to ask her if she was enjoying the show. But he decided that the humor value was not worth distracting Chong-kyu from the process at hand. And it was not long before she shuddered and murmured "Oh my gosh!". Al kissed her again. She looked at him, her cheeks a bit flushed, and said "Want a hand job, baby?"

"I'm fine. I came already."

"Here?"

"No, silly, when you gave me the blow job on top of the police car."

"Oh, yes, of course. That was fun, huh?"

"That would be putting it mildly…"

Chong-kyu said nothing more. She just kissed him and turned her attention back to the stage.

The performers had changed positions again. The young lady was sitting between them sucking first one then the other, and pumping both the whole time with her hands. Finally she stopped sucking and just said "Come on, you studs, give it to me!" she pumped them a few more times. The black haired man came hard onto her face. The blond haired man shot a huge load onto her breasts. The crowd cheered and the lights went down.

"I doubt we'll see anything to top that!" Chong-kyu said.

"Don't be too sure…" Darla countered "Look at her!"

Chong-kyu looked back at the stage. The woman walking into the light was wearing nothing but a tight ARMY t-shirt. Her black hair hung down to where her waist flared to perfectly proportioned hips that in turn led to strong shapely legs. Her skin was a golden color that made her black almond shaped eyes stand out. She led her man by the hand. He was tall and lean and also wearing a tight ARMY t-shirt.

"OK, let's stay for one more…" she agreed. She also gave Al's johnson an squeeze. "Look's familiar, huh, baby?" she whispered in his ear.

Al nodded and began rubbing her pussy again.

The lady in the Army t-shirt began dancing. As before, the man stood to the side, out of the spot light, slowly stroking his member as he watched her dance. And, as before, people hardly noticed him, they were staring at his lady, who danced divinely. As the first song ended, the man let go of his now mostly hard Johnson, walked off stage, and returned with a high padded stool which he set in the middle of the stage. The lady turned her back to the audience, set her feet apart so her legs were slightly spread, and leaned over the stool so her ass was up. She looked over her shoulder at the audience with a mischievous look on her face and began rubbing her pussy. The look on her face turned from one of mischief to one of delighted pleasure. When her man began kissing and kneading her ass checks she opened her mouth and began moaning. She reached out her free hand, grasped his erection, and began stroking it. She pulled him forward, guiding him into her mouth. She continued playing with her pussy with her right hand, bring her left down to massage her back door as she sucked. The man placed his hands on her head to steady it, and began thrusting in her mouth. She was clearly excited by it; the urgency of her moans increased. The man let go of her head, but she kept sucking with greater energy as she got more and more overcome by pleasure and excitement. Finally she opened her mouth and howled with a powerful orgasm. When the man pulled out of her mouth, moved around behind her, and entered her pussy she was hit by another orgasm, then another and another. She came in wave after wave as he thrust inside her. She screamed over and over as she came until she finally slumped over the stool, exhausted. Her man carried her over to a mattress on the stage and lay her gently down on it. She took his erection and guided it into her mouth again. She sucked slowly and dreamily. She let it go and rolled onto her side. The man rubbed lube onto his erection and lay down beside and behind her. She began rubbing her pussy with her right hand, using her left to guide him to her back door. He slowly pressed his way in. She leaned her head back and let out a great groan of pleasure. He thrust slowly in her back door. With each thrust her groans became stronger. Soon she was calling out "Oh, honey, oh…oh!" She shuddered and gushed with one last tremendous orgasm. He man pulled slowly out of her back door. He scooted around as he stroked his erection. He positioned himself over her face. She opened her mouth wide. He groaned and shot a tremendous load, coming on her cheek bones and into her mouth. When he finished coming, which took a surprisingly long time, he took her in his arms and carried her off stage.

The house lights came up. The DJ said something about the end of the last show…you don't have to go home but you can't stay here…and other foolishness. Anyway, it was time to go. Chong-kyu rose unsteadily to her feet. Al realized that his hand, and her crotch, were soaked. He looked at her. She smiled sheepishly. "…sorry…" she said.

Al just smiled, shook his head, and kissed her.

They walked out doors. Dawn was breaking. Darla and Ralph were staying at a place nearby, but Al and Chong-kyu's hotel was across town, so they said so long there.

It was a bit of a walk, but the early morning calm and coolness was refreshing. They walked arm in arm, just enjoying each other's company.

By the time they got back to the hotel, they realized they had just about enough time to get packed and get to the station to catch their train.

It was only late morning, but they were tired from staying up all night, so Al folded the bed down. They climbed into bed, snuggled up together and drifted off to sleep.

The afternoon sun streaming in the window woke him up. Al disengaged from Cheryl. As on the way down he made his way to the men's room at the front of car to get cleaned up.

When he returned to the room he found it empty. He lay back in the bed thinking of all the fun they'd had on their brief Mardi Gras visit. He smiled. He could feel himself getting hard, just thinking of some of the wild times. He was slowly, absently mindedly stroking his erection when Cheryl entered the roomette.

"Is that for me, baby?" she asked happily.

"Naturally" Al replied.

"Nice!" she said. She dropped her bag on the bed, grabbed Al's erection, and began going down on him.

"Wow!" Al said.

Cheryl kissed for a while. Then she raised her head. "Hey, baby, we really, really smell like sex. I think we better wash up. Is there any place on the train with a shower?"

"Not really…but we could give each other sponge baths from the sink."

"Oooh, sounds like fun."

"Mmmm, should be fun…after some play time?"

"Maybe we better get cleaned up now…if we fall asleep again and run out of time it could be…awkward."

"OK, fair enough."

"Sorry to leave you with a hard on. I promise I'll take care of it after."

 Al just chuckled and nodded. He wasn't going to complain. He knew Cheryl would more than make up for it. She always did.

They filled the sink with warm water. They used the hand towels first to wet each other down, then to soap each other, and finally to rise off in stages. They had to dump and refill the water in the sink several times. It was all great fun, especially because Cheryl insisted on kissing Al's erection every time it got anywhere near her face. Al, of course kissed Cheryl's pussy, breasts and shapely derriere every chance he got. Once they were clean and dry, they lay side by side kissing and cuddling. Cheryl grabbed Al's erection and started stroking. "You like it, baby?" she asked playfully.

"Oh, Chong-kyu, you know I do." He answered. He reached between her legs and began rubbing her pussy. He really enjoyed rubbing her pussy, it was such a pretty pussy.

Chong-kyu sat up, swung around, straddled Al's head, and sat on his face. Al began kissing her pussy with great enthusiasm. She bent down and started sucking him. They did a 69 that was tremendous fun for a while. Soon Chong-kyu was starting to breathe hard. She took Al's erection out of her mouth and leaned forward so she could moan and groan. "Oh, my gosh!" she gasped, shaking quickly. She stroked his erection, bent down and started licking his balls. Al had to stop kissing so he could let out a tremendous groan of pleasure. Chong-kyu wheeled around, straddled his hips, and lowered herself down onto his erection. Al reached up and rubber her breasts as she ground her hips and rode him to a series of wonderful orgasms. She threw her head back and howled as a particularly strong one shot through her. She collapsed on top of him and they rolled over. Al drove deep inside her. "Oh, Chong-kyu…Oh, Chong-kyu…I love you so…" he whispered urgently in her ear.

"I love you too, Al. I love you so much!" she answered. Then she couldn't talk because she was overwhelmed as another orgasm shook her. Al slowed to catch his breath. He kissed her face.

"Hey, baby…" Chong-kyu asked "want to try a little back door?"

"Sure! What made you think of that?"

"It just seemed like it would be fun…"

Al nodded. He slid back out of her. Chong-kyu rolled over and got up on her hands and knees. Al pressed slowly into her back door. "Wow…" he said.

"Mmm, fun!" Chong-kyu said.

Al began thrusting slowly and Chong-kyu moaned happily. He reached around between her legs and began rubbing her pussy. She let out a long sigh "Oh, baby, that's so goooood!"

Al continued rubbing her pussy, and Chong-kyu began gasping. "Oh, Al…Oh, Al, baby… Oh, AL!" she called out and gushed with an orgasm.

"Oh, Chong-kyu!" Al cried. He shook and came hard. He leaned over her, panting, his erection still in her ass. "Oh, Chong-kyu…."

"Oh, Al…Al, baby, that was awesome!"

Al just nodded. He kissed the back of her neck. He slowly withdrew. He made his way unsteadily to the sink, still breathing hard, and got two more wet wash cloths so they could get cleaned up.

"Looks like we need to wash all over." He observed.

"I suppose so…but worth it, right?"

"Oh…yes!"

After washing, they went to the dining car to get dinner. They talked about when they might meet again. Atlanta looked hopeful. There was also a trade show in New Jersey. But what looked best was a vacation together in Daytona Beach, Florida.

They brought a couple of beers back to the roomette. They lay in bed looking at the night time scenery passing sipping their beers. They didn't talk much. At some point, they drifted off to sleep.

In the morning Al was hoping to make love, but they were almost in Chicago by that time. "Next time, baby!" Cheryl assured him.

Al nodded. They had a long hug. Time for Al to go back to his seat in the coach.

Al stepped into the corridor, turned and started walking toward the back of the train to find a coach seat. The feeling of absence now that he was no longer holding Chong-kyu was almost a physical sensation, like a dull ache coupled with a sense of longing. It would pass, he knew, but it was still a bit overwhelming. As he made his way back to the coach, he alternated between trying to think of Zoe, and trying to hold onto the sense of the incredible Mardi Gras trip. Life was good, he knew.

For her part, Cheryl (she must think of herself a Cheryl now, not Chong-kyu) pulled her knees up and hugged her legs. She resisted the urge to call Al back for one more hug. She had to get her head straight for her reunion with Brad. And there would be more visits together, Atlanta if all went well, and others later. She stood up and started rechecking her bags to be sure everything was there. Activity was the best way to refocus her mind.

When the train pulled into the station, they exited the train at different locations. Al walked farther back until he found a set of stairs up from the platform to the station. As agreed, Cheryl walked forward to the stairs at the other end of the platform.

At the top of the stairs Cheryl spotted Brad. She trotted forward, dropped her bags when she was close and threw herself into his arms. He lifted her up and swung her around in celebration. It was good to be home. She'd had a great trip in so many ways, but it was good to be home. Back to sanity. She could hardly believe the stuff she did when she was with Al, especially when he started calling her Chong-kyu. She'd never done that stuff with anyone else, never wanted to, but for some reason with Al things went crazy. She could not have explain why, if anyone asked her. Anyway, best to set the thoughts aside for now. Brad was carrying her bags and asking if she was in the mood for some coffee before driving home. He was such a sweetie.

Al had not intended to, but he caught a glimpse of Brad and Cheryl's reunion. A bolt of jealousy flashed through him, but he got over it just as quickly. She was happy. That was important to him, he could not be happy if she were miserable. Besides, he was on his way home to Boston and Zoe. She was a good woman, and fun too. Not quite wild like Cheryl, her idea of an exhibitionist rush was playing the violin in the nude while Al watched. He smiled at the thought; it was a lovely sight.

Atlanta fell through, much to their disappointment. They met in New Jersey during the trade show, but only managed an hour and a half together; fun but limited. But then in January, because tickets just before the spring rush were cheap, they succeeded in taking a weekend in Daytona Beach together. They didn't manage to get a tan, but they did manage to…well, you can use your imagination.